SCARS

Terri Pray

Warning

This book contains sexually explicit scenes and adult language and may be considered offensive to some readers. Scars is for sale to adults ONLY, as defined by the laws of the country in which you made your purchase. Please store your books wisely, where they cannot be accessed by under-aged readers.

* * * * *

Published by Under the Moon, LLC
Pelican Rapids, MN

This book is a work of fiction. Any resemblance to actual events, locales or persons, living or dead, is completely coincidental.

Scars
ISBN: 978-1-938339-19-6
Copyright © 2015 Terri Pray
Cover Art Copyright @ 2018 Samuel Pray
Editor in Chief: Terri Pray
All rights reserved.

Scars

Praise for the writing of Terri Pray

Focused On Love is an absolute page-turner. The poignant heart-tugging characters touch the heart in such a way that it is hard releasing them once the book is finished. Dani and Steven make such a delightful couple and the way they seek to conquer the odds stacked up against them is well-written. Ms. Pray pens a sharp and intense read that keeps the reader mesmerized.
 -- Linda L., *The Romance Studio,* on *Focused On Love* (Magic Carpet Books)

Ettore's Women is a beautifully written and perhaps deliberately fragmented story of women who work in a brothel. Terri Pray's voice fascinates me. I want to read more.
 -- Catherine H., *Novelspot,* on *Ettore's Woman* (Extasy Books)

The novel flows extremely well. There is never a dull moment and the sex is blistering hot. *Sweet Deceptions* is a great way to spend a lazy afternoon. Full of intrigue it keeps you wondering what is happening and who did it.
 -- Leyna, *Fallen Angel Reviews,* on *Sweet Deceptions* (Magic Carpet Books)

...[A]n enjoyable fast read with the premise of being able to unleash the magic within yourself, if you have enough faith.
 -- Aggie Tsirikas, *Just Erotic Romance Reviews,* on *Green Dreams* (Extasy Books)

Dedication

To my Sam, thank you now and always for your help, love and support.

Chapter One

"This isn't about you; it's me." Kyle didn't even have the guts to look directly at her. He never did. Not even when his temper was at its full height. "I've tried to talk to you about this before, the differences between us I mean, but you wouldn't listen."

And he wanted to say it wasn't about her, but him, and then in the next breath he blamed her for not listening. Typical. He hadn't changed, no matter how much she had hoped he would, or the years of working with him. Wasted years. "I suppose you're going to tell me now that we can remain friends, or is that supposed to be my line?"

"Lines, is that what you think I'm doing, throwing you lines?"

"Isn't that what you always do? Use whatever lines you think will get you out of trouble this time?" Simone smiled despite the tension that built across her shoulders. Confrontations, no matter how used to them she had become, were still uncomfortable to deal with. "Or perhaps you'd prefer me to say that it really is better this way for both of us, or that it was really all my fault for not listening to you. Ah no, I have it. I should have known better than to become involved with a piece of low-life, double-talking, cheating scum like you."

"What?" Color drained from his face, eyes widening at her words.

"Did you think that I didn't know just what was going on this time? About Megan, Lisa, and what was the other woman's name last night, or did you ever even ask her name before you fucked her in our bed?" Better, this was so much better than just standing there taking shit from him again. She'd waited too long to face him down over this.

And by the look on Kyle's face, this had been the last thing he had expected from her.

"You've no idea what you're talking about. Have you been

hitting the bottle, or was it the pills this time?" He finally stammered out the accusations.

"You bastard. I've been clean for over five years." Her fists clenched at her sides, the urge to lash out, to damage that oh-too-perfect face built within her. "No matter what you've done to me, I've stayed away from those damn things, cut them out of my life, just as I'm cutting you out of my life now. You're a drug, a dangerous addiction. I've known that for months now."

"You're dumping me?" Shock registered across his face, outrage following a heartbeat later. "You can't dump me; I'm leaving you."

"You can't leave someone if they're already packed and ready to walk out." She gestured toward the waiting bags. Suitcases he had somehow missed when he had begun his diatribe. Did he really believe that he and he alone had the right to end the relationship? Of course he did. "My cab should be here any minute now."

"Where do you think you're going to go? You're nothing without me. You know that." He didn't move except for his stunned gaze that flickered from her bags back to her face. "You've got no where to go! I forbid you to leave. I won't permit it."

"Are you so sure that I have no where to go? And, since when did I become a piece of property for you to order around at your whim? I am far stronger than you ever thought I could be, Kyle." Good, he didn't know. All those weeks of planning, making arrangements, getting her papers, her things together, had paid off. Looking back, she doubted he'd even noticed the slow disappearance of her worldly possessions. "I've got myself a new job, an apartment, the start of a new life all without you."

For a moment he didn't speak, he didn't even try to, just a long slow look around the room, lingering on spots that had once held her small things as realization sank in. All her pictures were gone. Her diploma. That small carved piece of crystal her brother had sent her from some distant country that she'd been too drunk to remember when she'd been given the gift in the first place. Everything packed away, already spirited from sight into the protection of her suitcases.

"How long have you been planning this?"

"Long enough to know it's the right thing to do."

"Right for us?"

"No, for me." Selfish perhaps, but she was through being his safe warm place to return to when he was done with his latest fling. It had taken her long enough. Too long, her brother would have said had he lived to see her make the mistakes that had brought her to this point. "There is no us. There hasn't been for a very long time."

"Selfish bitch. After everything I've given you, all the support. I put a roof over your head, gave you food and comfort. I helped you through the darkness every time you slipped."

"You lying sack of shit. Helped me? You pushed me into the mire every damn chance you got. Any time I spoke out against you, tried to get you to see something, you'd accuse me of drinking, or hitting the pills. You put the bottle into my hands a dozen times in the past month alone. I didn't take a single mouthful, not even with the bottle in my hand. Did you even notice that at the time? No, of course you didn't. You're all too willing to look for the weaknesses and yet you ignore any form of strength I try to show." Her hands clenched tighter, skin taut across her knuckles, nails biting into her palms. "You tried to kill me, little by little every single damn day I didn't bow down to your wishes, or look the other way with your petty little games. You haven't touched me in a loving way in over a year."

"What the hell are you talking about? We did it only last week." His gaze narrowed on her face. "Twice in fact."

"A few grunts and moans as you roll my way and try to fuck me without letting me wake up is not a loving way. Self-centered bastard. It's all you've ever been. I was just too afraid to admit it to myself until recently."

Darkness claimed his gaze, lines tightening about his eyes. "Scar-faced slut. With how you look you should be grateful any man touches you at all."

It should have hurt, the words were meant to lash into her soul, tear out her heart, and leave her a sobbing heap on the floor.

"That's the funny thing about waking up one day and realizing the man you're with is nothing more than a spoiled child willing to lash out at anyone in order to get what he wants. One day those words simply cease to have any meaning." Simone smiled, bending down enough to pick up her bags. His words had long since lost any power where she was concerned. A pity it had taken so long before she had been able to see it for herself. "I think I finally came to understand that in order for words to hurt, they have to be spoken by someone who means something to me. And you, my dear, ceased to mean anything to me a long time ago."

She saw it, the warning flashing across his eyes before the growl left his lips. The danger signs she knew far better than she had ever wanted to. But this time, yes this time she was ready for him. By the time his fist came up toward her face, she'd dropped the bags and stepped out of the way, enough that he stumbled forward. Anger left him clumsy.

"I'm giving you fair warning. You ever lay or try to lay a hand on me again, I'll call the cops on you. I've taken enough from you; it's not happening again. Not this time, not ever again. Do you understand me?" No raised voices, no threats of violence against him, just the cold hard facts of what his actions would bring. "I have the number programmed into my cell phone, and the doctor has all the necessary medical reports at hand from your previous attacks. And believe me, I will turn them all over. You'd be faced with a long and uncomfortable jail sentence. Perhaps you might find a nice boyfriend to keep you company."

For one brief moment, she could imagine the look on his face when he found himself in a cell with his new boyfriend.

Scars

"You wouldn't dare." He snarled, turning to face her, eyes dark as the pits themselves.

"A week ago you would have said the same thing about me packing up and leaving. Take a good look around you before you declare what I would and would not dare to do." Keep calm. As long as she kept calm, he couldn't win, couldn't find a crack in her armor to poke through. No, she'd closed them all. This time he'd be the one standing there as she walked through the door, standing there staring and wondering just what happened in order for him to lose his grip on the power.

He'd never understand.

He didn't want to even try to see things from her viewpoint. She was there. A part of his life, one he had the right to walk away from and expect to find her waiting for his return. A good and loyal little pet.

No longer.

"Bitch."

She smiled, collected the bags from the floor, and walked toward the door without so much as looking back at him. If that's all he had, then she was safe. Her simple decision had rendered him as helpless as a toddler throwing his first temper tantrum.

Exactly how he had managed to make her feel for far longer than she wanted to remember ...

* * * * *

"I can't believe you pulled this off. You really managed to do it, after all this time?" Mandy pushed a mug of hot chocolate into Simone's hands, the mug piled high with rapidly melting cream. "I was worried you'd back out."

"I've backed up so much in the past couple of years that I really don't think I had anywhere left to go." The mug should have felt warm, but she still felt numb. Despite the show of courage when she'd faced Kyle down, she'd been a shaky, nervous wreck a moment after the cab door had closed, her bags in the trunk.

"I would've killed to have been a fly on the wall when you stood up to him." Mandy flopped down into the overstuffed couch, curling her feet up beneath her. "He's been needing a good taking down for the last year or longer. Bastard. He wouldn't know a good woman if he was given a damn road map and a set of instructions."

Simone nearly dropped the mug, choking back a laugh. Gods, she had needed that.

"It's true and you know it. Now, the question is, what will you do next?"

"I don't know. Not really. I can't stay in town. He's not the sort to just let matters drop." There lay the real problem. Kyle didn't give up. It was one thing for him to dump her, but he'd never let her just walk out of his life with the upper hand. Not when he'd been expecting to come back to her within a week, or less if he'd run true to form. "I have that job to go to, but I'm not due to start there for a few more weeks."

"I can't believe he called you a scar-faced slut. That man ... no, he's not a man; he's a boy who never grew up." Her friend scowled, setting down her own mug. "I'd like to take a baseball bat to his head."

"He wouldn't be worth the effort." She murmured, running her fingers over the scars that marked the left-hand side of her face. She'd learned to hide the worst of it under a good makeup, but the raised ridges refused to sink back into her cheek. Sometimes she could ignore they were there, until she caught the horrified, stunned looks from those who dared to actually visually admit that they had seen the marks on her face.

"Oh, love, don't let him get to you. It doesn't matter about a few scars. They don't make you who you are. They're just a part of the outside. It's nothing more than window dressing. Anyone who takes even a few minutes to talk to you, to get to know you, learns to see past them."

Scars

She wanted to believe that, but too often she saw where people's gazes were fixed on that first meeting. The mess that remained of that side of her face, the scars that marched across her cheek in violent claw-like marks, ripping a path back toward her ear. She barely remembered the dog now. Just the snapping, growling. Those horrid noises. Even now she couldn't go anywhere near dogs.

Three years old, an autumn night that had been too mild to close the window. Moonlight had filtered into her bedroom by the edge of the lake. Distant sounds, peaceful until the dog had jumped into her room.

She didn't even realize that she was shaking until the sound of the mug clattering on the large saucer snapped her out of the memory.

"Simone, don't think about. You're not that child anymore. You didn't deserve that type of remark from him, or anyone else."

Scar face, hag, slut, ugly bitch. She'd heard all of that and more over the years. It didn't matter that she hadn't done anything to trigger the attack, or that she took every precaution to hide the marks, she still caught the looks, the narrowed gazes, those quick indrawn breaths when people realized that they were real and not just a figment of their imaginations.

"I've thought of going home earlier than required for work." She'd lied to Kyle about the apartment and the job. The job wasn't much; well, it would pay a small wage, enough so she didn't have to rely on her father for everything.

"Home? You haven't been back there in six years. I still don't understand just why you took a job there instead of staying here."

"Longer. I haven't been back since Mom died." Not even to see her Dad. "Kyle would look for me if I stayed local. He'd hound me, given half the chance. I don't want that. I need to break away from him fully."

"I thought ... never mind." Mandy lost her train of thought, falling silent for a moment. "Okay, do you need to tell anyone you'll be going home?"

"There's no one else I have to tell." Her dad wouldn't care if she just turned up. He probably wouldn't even notice. No letters, calls. She'd tried over the years and slowly lost hope that he would ever acknowledge that she still lived. So why go back?

A dozen and more reasons came to mind. She owned the house, knew the area. The local police wouldn't stand for Kyle getting in the way, even if he did find out where she had gone. She missed the peace and quiet of the area.

Truth be known, there was only one reason.

It was home.

Chapter Two

The small town hadn't changed, nor had the cabin and her father. Well, he'd looked up when she'd walked into the kitchen -- then he'd nodded and gone right back to doing his crossword puzzles. Time had added a few more grey hairs to his head and the lines around his eyes had become a little deeper, but the noncommittal grunts, shrugs, and occasional mumbled greetings first thing in the morning had all remained the same.

Three weeks of the same noncommittal noises, then an uncomfortable silence followed by what could've been a muttered word or three before he'd crawl right back into his puzzle books. He didn't even care that she owned the cabin, just as long as she left him alone. At first the silence had been welcome, time she could recover from living in a large city, settle, and shut out the memory of Kyle's cruel words.

What did she need the cabin for?

The road of her life had taken her to the cities, in search of something -- she had forgotten just what dreams had danced before her eyes on that first trip away from home. Time had left them little more than shadowed and unwanted memories.

Kyle. A poor choice for which she now paid the price.

Had it left her stronger, or just more understanding of who she was and the world that existed beyond the cabin?

Time alone would tell.

She glanced up for a brief moment, her gaze moving over the small but welcoming diner. How often had she spent Saturday here? More than she wanted to count. The library and the path down by the river had been the other favorite getaway locations.

Funny how easy it had been to fall back into old habits.

A good cup of coffee, the newspaper, and some time away from the cabin had been sorely needed. Cabin fever? Not really. More a case of the hundreds of memories that had begun to batter down on her limited defenses. Her mother, old friends, those were the ones she had been able to cope with. But the others, the night with the dog followed by weeks in the hospital and years of pain. The facial exercises she'd had to do in order to stop her face from tightening up. They'd been almost too much to cope with.

Faces, some familiar, others new to her. Bodies taking up space in the booths, at the counter, and the few real tables in the diner. Some low conversation, but nothing that stood out.

She could fade into the background for a time. Soak up the atmosphere as she tried to adjust to the quieter and slower pace of small town life.

Had the staff changed?

One of the waitresses looked vaguely familiar, but she couldn't be sure.

The newspaper flicked open with a light touch. Nothing major. A few deaths, a couple births, and a marriage announcement or two from local families, the sort of get-together that would bring half the townspeople together for the party afterwards. No murders or thefts, just a report of someone arrested for drunk and disorderly behavior. A dozen reports on crop prices, land, farms changing hands.

A slight smile tugged at the corners of her lips. It was odd, not seeing any reports of major crime. Not that the town would always be this peaceful, but she wasn't about to complain. Unless something major happened, such as three gangs moving in, or world war breaking out, the biggest excitement would remain the out-of-town speeders and the local boys having a little too much to drink at the wrong moment.

Malts. Hadn't she drowned her sorrows a time or two with a malt here? Mint and Oreo malts, double thick, with cream on top that she had to eat with a spoon. The sort of drink that meant you didn't have to bother with a meal for some time.

Something to indulge in another time.

Scars

"Simone? Simone Hawkins? Is that really you?" His voice cut through her daydreams as no other could have done.

Hazel eyes, flecked with touches of gold, a deep smile that curled the corners of his lips. That quirky look that had broken the hearts of a dozen girls growing up, including her own, though she'd fought to hide it from him. What good would it have done to let him know she had fallen for him back then? She would've just been one of many, and it would have given weapons to others at school. No, far better that she had kept it hidden.

He was still far too handsome for his own good -- his face, the play of muscles under his work shirt, the cut of his jeans that left little to the imagination. Her gaze took a slow path down his chest, lingering along his belt before briefly skimming across the line of the bulge that beckoned her gaze.

Dammit. She knew better than to look at a man as if he were nothing more than a piece of meat. What was it about him? He still left her feeling like a school girl with her first crush, but as long as he never found out, she could live with that. "Victor?"

"I thought for a minute that I was seeing things, but it's really you. Gods. Okay, that sounded lame." He chuckled, shifting his weight from foot to foot.

So much for the smooth boy she recalled from high school. He'd always been so confident, and now he stood there, awkward, uncertain of himself and expecting to be sent away. Had he been slapped down a time or two since she'd left home? The thought was almost unimaginable. "Are you going to stand there all day, or join me? There's plenty of room."

Where had that come from? She'd never had the nerve to ask someone to join her before. At least not that she could remember. Maybe breathing the fresh air and shaking off the taste of the city had actually done her some good after all?

Or the strength that had finally pushed her to walk out on Kyle.

Whatever the cause she wasn't about to dissect it now.

"I was thinking of getting a cup of coffee, and if you wouldn't mind, I'd love to join you." He gestured toward the opposite side of the booth.

Her heart skipped a beat. Even faltering, that moment where he'd seemed unsure, she'd felt the old pull toward him. Who was she trying to kid? They'd all felt it. Every girl at school had dreamed about him, tried to find a way to date him. Out of all of them, only she'd held back. Why would he want anything to do with her, the scar-faced freak, when he'd had perfect tens to choose from?

Stupid.

He'd only asked to be polite, to welcome an old school companion back home, or something of that nature. No matter how he looked, or the surge of delight she felt as his gaze moved from the spare seat to her eyes and back again, she had to keep in mind that a man like him would never give her the time of day, at least not in a romantic way.

Screw romance, she'd have been happy with a good hard fuck with a man who, if the high school rumors were to be believed, knew just how to treat a woman.

Heat flushed a path across her cheeks. This wasn't high school, and it was just a cup of coffee.

"No, please feel free to." She gestured toward the seat opposite, trying to avoid meeting his eyes. They could have held her gaze for eternity and she'd have died a happy woman. Her nipples crinkled, pressing taut points against the thin summer shirt she wore, a damp wave rippling through the lining of her sex, thighs pressing tight together in the hope he didn't see, didn't sense her growing arousal.

Dammit, after all these years he could still do that to her.

"Where have you been? You vanished what, eight, nine years ago. Wasn't that just after your Mom died?"

"About then," she murmured.

"What happened to you?" He waved over the waitress,

ordering a cup of coffee and a hamburger, rare. "You just left town without telling anyone where you were going."

What had he wanted, an announcement taken out in the paper?

She hadn't been needed, and she doubted anyone had really noticed she'd left, despite the concern she could hear in Victor's voice.

"I had no reason to stay and every reason to leave." The world had waited for her, beckoned her away from what she now knew to be the safety of her hometown. False promises of a good life, work, decent men and women who could look past her face into her heart. Instead, she'd stumbled and found that the only person who could bring her back out of the pits that had drawn her in had been herself.

"And yet you came home."

"I had no reason to stay away." She admitted with a slight shrug.

"Interesting," he glanced back to check for the waitress. Good, his attention was wandering. Another few minutes, and he'd offer a stilted farewell before finding an excuse to leave.

"What is?" She gave a quick look around. "Is there something wrong?"

Go on, say it. That you're busy and have to leave. Or you just remembered you have a business meeting to attend. Some hot date waiting for you a hundred miles from here.

"Nothing, sorry. I wasn't sure what else to say there." Victor smiled, looking back at her, hands folded in front of him on the table. "You left because you had no reason to stay and came back because you had no reason to stay away. Forgive me if this sounds rude, but it sounds as though you've not really been that sure what to do since you left home."

"I guess." Heat rose in twin spots on her cheeks. Gods, he must have thought she was lame, or just plain stupid.

"Who was he?"

"He?" She looked up.

"There had to have been a boyfriend, fiancé or lover, maybe a husband in the time you've been gone. Though I'm betting that's a no on the husband side of things. I can't see any sign of a ring, or a band from one." He nodded toward her hands.

"Kyle. His name was Kyle, and he was no one special." She shrugged, trying to avoid his eyes. The last thing she needed to do was spill out her guts to the high school heartthrob. Besides, he had to be married or dating, or both. If the rumors from old times had been even remotely true, then Victor had always had at least two women on the go, sometimes more, and no one minded.

Men like him were allowed to break, bend, and rewrite the rules on a whim.

"Something happened between you two?" He leaned against the table, trying to look directly into her eyes. Why did he want to do that? Did she have something on her face?

"Too many things and none of them good," she admitted before stopping to think about it. "I'm sorry. You don't want to hear about my life." Just why was he asking questions like that anyway?

A bet? A dare? Gods, there had to be some reason why he was paying her so much attention. Unless he did actually like her and want to know what was going on with her life. Who was she trying to kid? If he had a reason to be interested in her, it wouldn't be a good one, knowing her luck.

Only things had changed.

Simone slumped. The courage to return home and the way she'd invited Victor to sit down with her for a coffee. She wasn't the same woman she had been all those years ago.

"If I didn't, I wouldn't have asked." Victor spoke softly, a warmth reflected in his eyes. Gods, he hadn't changed that much, except in ways that made him even more handsome and twice as compelling as she'd remembered. "So tell me about him, about you."

Chapter Three

Simone. Damn the last person he had expected to walk into today had been her. After all those years, she'd finally returned home. The whys didn't really matter that much, though he probed gently for information and tried to draw the young woman out of her shell. She still acted like she was half afraid he'd bite her, and with good reason.

The scars. They'd faded a little over the years, but he knew every line of them. They'd been burned into his mind for a lifetime.

For a moment he could see it as if it had happened yesterday.

The hunt. He'd been so young and eager, but even then he'd known going near the cabin had been wrong. The pack wouldn't listen, not to a cub, and Simone had paid the price. That damn Rogue had tried to prove himself the strongest of all his age mates. And how better to prove it than to dare to go into the cabin and try to take out one of the humans there? The male had been the target.

Simone's father.

Now there had been a human worth hunting, at least in his prime. A hunter, tracker, a man of the forest in many ways. If he had been one who had threatened the pack, then Victor would have understood why they had gone after the man.

Because he had been there, foolish, but the reasons boiled down to just that. A foolish idea and Simone had paid the price.

So much blood, yet no one had died. It had tainted the air, called to him and the rest of the pack. Screams, he could still hear the screams of the child. The girl. Three, no, four years old. So brave, brandishing a pillow at the wolf, screaming for the doggy to go away, get out, leave her alone. Not even pack members could have shown such courage at that age, yet she'd remained there, refusing to back down, even with the blood streaming from her face.

He glanced up at the woman she had become, the marks on her face that she would carry for the rest of her life.

His fault. If he'd not tormented Craig, then the attack would never have taken place. Life in the pack was never easy for secondary alphas. As the son of the leader, the eldest of the cubs, he should have known better, yet he'd pushed and the child had paid the price.

A child no longer though, a woman's body, soft eyes, a gentle voice and a hidden, untapped strength that glimmered behind the fragile shield she wore. What would it be like to pull her into his arms? To smell her body pressed against his? Would she have melded to him, or growled and fought back, struggling to retain some level of dominance?

Was that arousal he could smell? Faint, too subtle a scent for a normal human nose to pick up on, but his body knew and responded in kind, a throb rushing through his cock, thickening it, pressing it tight against his jeans.

Don't stand up. She'd be able to see it. As long as he didn't stand up he'd be safe from embarrassment.

"He hurt you then?" She'd fallen silent halfway through her tale of the man she had left. "The one you left behind?"

"In more ways than one, though I should have left him years back." Simone met his gaze for a brief moment before looking away, heat burning in her cheeks. A veil of dark hair brushed over her face, shielding her eyes from his gaze. "He loved me, once ... I think. I used to think that, at least; now I'm not so sure he ever knew what love was."

"Men don't hurt someone they love." He'd never hurt her, would he? No, he'd seen what some men managed to do, but they didn't love the women they beat, or tossed aside, or left to cry curled up in a ball in a back room somewhere.

Had he hit her?

He struggled to prevent a frown from creasing his brow. The

thought of some man raising his hand to any woman -- no, more so with this woman -- left him fighting back a rage that burned within him.

Those who did certain things deserved a long and very slow death.

"Men do exactly what they want, when they want, and to hell with the consequences." A fire blazed within her soft green eyes. "You know that better than most, Victor. How many hearts have you broken since high school? How many did you destroy then?"

"What?" He nearly choked on the sip of coffee. "What are you talking about? I didn't break any hearts. I'm not like that."

"Yes, you did, every time you kissed a woman and then left her for the next one. How many did you do more than kiss before you dropped them on the wayside?" Her knuckles turned white, her grip tight about the mug.

Fire, passion, fury, she raged against him, against men like him. Or the man she thought he was. How could he make her see that he just wasn't like that?

Her lips pursed together, a fury battling in her eyes, fear, unspoken betrayal that was far more than the little she had told him about. He wanted to move, gather her into his arms, curl her tight against his chest as he kissed away the tears she refused to let spill down her cheeks.

He had to make her see she was mistaken about him.

"I kissed and did little more than that with most. I might have had half the women in class hanging around, wanting to be the next girl of the moment, but I didn't take advantage of that. No matter what the rumors said, I didn't do things like that. I've never been the sort of man that would willingly hurt a woman." How could he explain to her that wolves mated for life? Better yet, how was he supposed to explain that he had the ability to change into a wolf in the first place? It wouldn't have made sense to her. Better to hope that she would believe his words, not ask for proof, and leave it at that.

"Why should I believe you? The talk had you in bed with thirty girls in the last year of school alone." Tiny lines around her eyes crinkled.

"And do you believe every rumor you hear?" He leaned in close, shoulders tensing, his gaze locking with hers. Wrong button to press, a reaction she didn't want to have to deal with, but she'd opened the door. Time for him to walk through it. "I'm sure the ones about you were far from true. How you were a witch, and that's why the dog ..."

Color drained from her face; the cup dropped to skitter across the table and crash against the floor, shattering.

"I'm sorry. I shouldn't have said that." How could he have been so cruel to her? Because he was stupid and had lashed out instead of taking a breath, thinking things through, and then opening his mouth wide enough to stick his foot into it. "Please, forgive me." He'd been just as abusive as the man she'd fled from. Heartless. When all he had wanted to do was protect her from the exact same wounds he had just inflicted on her aching soul.

She didn't speak. Her lips moved, but no sound reached his ears.

Cruel words, he should never have given them life. Pain shone in her eyes, held in crystalline form by unshed tears. Silently she shook her head, her lips pressed into a firm line, harsh, jaw set as she slipped out from behind the table walking away from him without ever giving life to the harsh words of revenge she would've had every right to spit at him.

With courage, grace, beauty, and a soft vulnerability that few women had ever displayed, Simone walked out of the diner, leaving the crumpled dollar bills on the counter to cover the cost of her coffee. Even in her hurt, she refused to be beholden to him.

Gods, what had he done?

Apart from act like a cub who didn't know any better.

Stupid.

You need her.

Scars

No, he didn't. Not Simone, not a woman who had never wanted anything to do with him and who now strode down the high street as quickly as her pride would permit her to without breaking into a full-fledged run.

Why deny it? You've wasted how many years shutting her out, the memory of those screams. Craig knew she was the one for you. That's why he attacked her, clawed her the way he did. Human reaction in wolf form, foolish really. As if a few scars matter to our kind.

Damn voice, the wolf, his other half, the true face of his soul if the voice was to be believed. It was ageless, ever wise beyond his years, and it was seldom ever silent. He was right. He needed Simone, wanted her. All those years he'd watched, hoped for the courage to make a move, to claim her, but the walls, the shield she had forced into place in order to survive had been a barrier as firm as the old Berlin wall.

If I remained silent, then how could I stop you from making such a fool of yourself? You know you want the girl, need her. Your father knew; Craig still knows. Do you think that rogue will just sit back and let her be claimed by you, or let her be ignored? He could take the entire pack with her.

She was just a woman, spirited, bright, bold, brave in so many ways, but still only a female. How could Craig take control of the pack by taking one woman for his mate? Besides, Craig was no longer a rogue, the pack had welcomed him back in after his exile. As much as any secondary alpha could be welcomed. The tension was ever present, but he had still been welcomed.

The same way you can be. She carries the bloodline and should have been brought over to us years ago, but you were determined to fight the call. The pack might have welcomed him back in, but that hasn't stopped the problems between you, has it?

Mates, what did he need with a mate, or cubs?

It's a part of our nature. We must breed. The lines must continue. To just sit back and let the pack die out would be a crime.

We missed one female, her mother, and now you would condemn the pack by ignoring the daughter? How many other females do you know that carry that scent? The ability to birth more of us?

None. They'd died or been killed, claimed by accidents. Only Simone had remained that he knew of. There would be others, elsewhere, well beyond the limits of the pack, but she was the only one he knew of who fell within the boundary claimed by his pack. Returning as she had done had to be a sign. Strange. When he'd stumbled across her scent, he'd denied it was her, allowed himself to believe that a different female had entered the town. Foolish. The rest of the pack would see it as such. They'd know soon enough, if they didn't already. They would have scented her as soon as she'd entered their hunting grounds. Craig would know. He'd only wait so long before claiming her for his own and taking the leadership of the pack along with his new mate.

Then they would fight.

No getting around it. The alpha with the right mate had the chance to take control of the pack. Great.

"I don't want to be the Alpha," he murmured into the coffee, ignoring the sideways look from the harried waitress. "I never wanted to be the pack alpha."

Oh, okay, well I'll just let Craig know. He can rip your throat out, claim the female and everything will be right with the world.

Chapter Four

Simone stalked down the high street, ignoring the sideways looks and outright stares that flashed her way. Her jaw clenched, teeth grinding against each other as her anger grew with each hurried step. Old stores, a few new ones, she barely noticed the changes. They could have put a superstore in the middle of the high street and she would have walked past it without so much as blinking, the way she now felt.

Bastard. He'd never change. Men never did. Always so smug, quick to lash out at others without giving even a moment's thought to how they'd feel afterwards. How she now felt.

How dare he?

What gave him the right to treat her like that? She'd done nothing to him. Nothing. Her comments, well everyone had thought that about him, hadn't they? Just as they'd called her a scar-faced hag, demon spawn, thrown masks at her during the year only to laugh and say she didn't need makeup or costumes at Halloween.

She wouldn't cry. No matter what he'd said, or the looks that still followed her through the town. She was stronger than that now, stronger than the little girl who had hidden in closets or behind the lockers, instead of facing the taunts that would be waiting for her on the way home from school.

They couldn't make her cry any longer.

Kyle had taught her what to do. His cruelty, the words, blows, and the slaps that knocked her to the floor. All of it had been nothing more than a practice run for this time, this moment, her return home, for this moment when she would face her past.

It wasn't fair. He could still turn her legs to jelly with a single look. Not that she'd let him know that. He'd never know, not as long as she lived. It wasn't as though he could read her mind.

Lying to herself -- she'd become good at that over the years.

Another set of walls to hide behind instead of letting others see just what she felt now, how she hurt. She'd taken that pain and turned it into brick and mortar, adding to the protections that she cowered behind. Odd how she could do that, how once the wall was in place she could pretend that the words meant nothing.

Simone faltered, catching a glimpse of her face in the shop window. Scars were just marks, lines, a road map of her life. Nothing to be afraid or ashamed of -- wasn't that what her mom had tried to tell her? She had earned them, through pain, fire, and fear. They were badges of honor, not marks of the petty hatred that others carried in their hearts.

Her fingers moved to the raised marks, tracing them, and for the first time she didn't shudder in revulsion. She'd changed. More than she had ever thought possible. No more the child, the cowering, blubbering creature behind the lockers.

It was time to rip down the walls.

"Simone?" A softer voice, a woman's, one she should have known if for no other reason than the slight mocking tone at the end of the word. "Is that really you? They said you'd come home but I didn't believe them. You know how quickly rumors spread in a town of this size."

Ann Welch. She hadn't changed in all the years Simone had been away. Dark hair, pale blue eyes, that quirky smile that left her feeling unsettled and that deep cold stare that fixed on the scars on Simone's face. "Well, they were right. I'm home."

"Why? It's not as though there's anything here for you."

"Isn't there?" She glanced back toward the diner and the faint image of Victor in one of the booths. "Funny, Victor seemed quite happy to see me again." She didn't have to tell Ann about the fight. Better to let the cold-faced woman believe the worst. If nothing else, the thought of them spending any time together would eat away at Ann's guts.

"Victor? He wouldn't have anything to do with you back then. Why would he now?" Tiny lines crinkled into life at the corners of

Scars

Ann's mouth.

"I guess you should ask him then; we've just shared a very pleasant lunch." Lies, but the look of shock that claimed Ann's face was worth the slight twist in her gut.

"Stupid slut, why would we want someone like you here? You're fooling yourself if you think Victor would want you. He was just taking pity on you." Ann smirked, one hand resting on her hip. "Even your pop doesn't want anything to do with you, does he? He can't stand to see the scars on your face. It drove your mom to her grave, seeing you all marked up like that. Of course, she must have blamed herself, or maybe she knew it was meant to be."

"Don't you have anything better to do with your life?" Simone glanced toward Ann's hands. No sign of a ring. Did she still pine for Victor? An evening spent with Craig had ruined any hopes of a relationship there. Her own fault, not that a woman like Ann would ever admit to that. "Or have you been hanging around street corners waiting for some chance to pounce on me with the same words you spouted at me back in school?"

Ann stuttered, giving a fair impression of a landed fish.

"No husband? Of course not. You're still hoping that Victor will forgive your indiscretions with Craig. Or, shall I put things a little more bluntly? Yes, why not. He still hasn't forgiven you for taking a long, hard fuck with Craig under the bleachers." Oh, she'd been waiting a long time to say that. Too long.

"Bitch," Ann hissed.

"Is that it? Is that all you can say to me after all these years? You've waited for years to spit your little lines at me and the best comeback you can come up with is calling me a bitch?" She fought the urge to laugh, but the smile tugged at the corners of her lips, a soft chuckle following on its heels. "Gods, I used to be so nervous of you and your little gang. Did you know that? But I can see it now. You're still nothing more than a high-school bully. Well, you're out of luck, Ann. You might not have grown up, but I have."

Damn, you can see them going at it. The warm voice growled at the back of his mind. *Interesting to see; you always thought she lacked backbone. Well, you're wrong. She stood up to that silly slut. I can't believe Ann still believes you might look her way.*

Why would he? The woman had slept her way through half of the football team. Even before he'd caught her with Craig, he'd already written her off as a lost cause. Double standards, he accepted that. Men were allowed, almost encouraged, to try out as many women as they could, but a woman who indulged in the same passions was just not suitable as a mate. Not an alpha mate, at least.

You knew back then that Simone was the woman you were meant to be with.

He wanted to shut the wolf side of his nature up, but the only way he could do that would be to find a ...

A what, a cure? Do you still think I'm just a disease? You know better than that. Do I have to go through the whole explanation again? I really thought you knew better than that.

Yes, he did. His other half, the spirit that helped him stay sane when the change hit him, whatever he wanted to call the voice, he couldn't be rid of it unless he found a way to tear the wolf side of his nature out of his being. And then he'd be nothing more than half a man.

What was the voice?

The spirit of the wolf would have been the easiest way of describing it. A voice, a guide he had heard since he had been a small boy. They all had one. Some were older, others younger, but they all tried their best to help the werewolves they had found themselves paired with.

You'd be lost without me.

True enough. At times the advice of the wolf spirit guide or whatever it was had been a great help. At others, well, an annoyance would've been putting it politely.

He peered out the window, watching the two women for

Scars

a moment longer, Ann still staring after the departing figure of Simone, her face flustered, red, hands clenched tight at her sides. She'd lost the fight, or so it seemed.

Good, the silly female needs to learn she's just a silly little bitch and not worth getting pups on. Not like Simone. You could lose yourself in her body. Did you see the way her nipples were standing out? I think she's in heat. You should go and pin her down now. It wouldn't take much just to lift her skirts. A few smooth words, a lingering kiss ... what, did I say something wrong again?

Victor bit back a remark, setting the money down on the counter as he headed out of the diner. Damn lupine voice. Didn't he know by now that humans mated for more than the call of a female in heat?

And she's definitely coming into heat.

A bitten tongue, that's what he'd end up with before the day was over. Just as well no one seemed to notice him these days, just as long as he kept his head down and out of the way of Craig.

That damn rogue would be the death of him one day.

No, not your death, but you'll have to face him down eventually.

Maybe he would, but not just yet. And not in the middle of the street. The struggle for control of the pack was coming. No, if he was going to be honest, it had been going on for years. Long before his father had died, before the attack on Simone's cabin. It was part of life as a shifter, werewolf, pack creature, alpha, whatever he wanted to call it.

At least humans were able to put on a front about sharing power. Pity it didn't work that way with his kind. The hormones, pheromones, whatever it was that got in the way seemed to be determined to prevent the pack structure from working without fights, without the struggle for power.

"Victor?"

Dammit, he should have waited until Ann had left before he'd walked out of the diner. He turned, meeting her gaze. "Yes?"

"I thought that was you. That Simone woman said you'd had lunch with her. Is that true?" Ann hurried over, heels clicking against the stone. Heels. Out here of all places. With the cracks in the sidewalk and the mud brought in by the pickup trucks and farmers, she was asking to end up on her backside. Didn't she have a grain of common sense?

It was all about appearances to Ann; it always had been.

"Yes, it is." He could have dropped Simone in it, but Ann deserved taking down a peg or two. "Why?"

"Oh, I ... well, why would you?"

"Why not? She's an old school friend. And besides, I thought you'd be glad to see her home again." He smiled, watching the shock register in Ann's gaze. A familiar scent coated her skin, teasing him with the knowledge of what she had been up to earlier in the day. "Was there anything else? I've got some work that I need to catch up with."

"Well, are you doing anything this evening? Mom's throwing one of her summer barbecues, and I'd love to see you there." Ann struggled to regain a little ground, shifting the conversation with little real skill. "I thought you could come swimming with me at the lake afterwards."

"Open invitation?" He smiled, a wicked idea gaining life at the back of his mind. Sex clung to her form, a subtle smell half hidden by the strong soap she'd used afterwards. Lavender? No something else. Fake flowers of some sort, mixed in a soap base.

"Yes, yes, of course. If you have a few friends you want to bring with you, I'd be delighted to meet them."

He doubted that, especially if he managed to turn up with Simone in tow. "What time is the party supposed to start?"

Sneaky, devious, designed to put her back in her place. I love it.

"Eight, but you can turn up any time you feel like it." Ann smiled, tracing one finger lightly over his arm. "I'll be there all night for you, and I'm sure we can find a few things to keep us busy after the meal and swimming session."

Scars

"I'm sure we can, but I'll have to see if I can be there first." And see if Simone would forgive him.

"Craig is going to be there; I thought I'd best warn you about that. I know you two don't get along very well." Ann leaned in against him as she tried to move into the circle of his arms. "There's nothing going on between him and me. You know that, don't you? There never has been. I know rumors spread very quickly through a town like this. Small lies designed to cause problems."

Sure, and you haven't spent the best part of the morning with Craig. Does she think you're blind? I can smell him on her. Silly little female.

He inhaled slowly, taking in the familiar scent of sex and Craig. His musk, her body; it wasn't that hard to figure out what they'd been doing. Had he bitten her? No, no, he wouldn't. Their kind refrained from biting females until there was an alpha for the pack.

Unless they really wanted to push an issue. He frowned, tempted for a moment to pull Ann close and search her for signs of the mark, a bite. Something. No, not even Craig would take it that far.

"Well, that could be interesting." Sure, if you thought that two alphas squaring off at a party could be classed as entertainment.

"Promise me you won't get into a fight with him, please." She whispered, trailing her fingers over his chest. "He only tries to make you jealous because he wants to be you."

In more ways than one.

"I know, he's always been like that." Sex, raw sex. Gods, it would have been so easy.

No. He wasn't going to make that mistake, not when Simone had returned.

That's the difference between you and Craig. You know you need a mate; Craig isn't ready to face that yet. If he marks a woman, claims her fully, he won't be able to fool around with the little bitches like this one.

Chapter Five

Mud slapped against the side of the truck, splattering against the bright red paint. She'd have to get it cleaned off again, but once a week was more than enough to wash the truck down, with the roads she had to use. Jaw tight, hands clenched on the wheel, trying to keep the truck on the dirt track that masqueraded as a road, she still simmered from Victor's remarks.

Still, she'd managed to slap Ann in the face, verbally at least. A physical slap might have offered more satisfaction, but Ann wasn't worth getting into trouble for. Not even after all the hurt the woman had caused Simone over the years.

Gods, why had she come home? No work, no boyfriend, and no real freedom. Her computer had arrived in one piece and the luxury of high speed had been replaced with the sluggish half-on-half-off connection of the local dial-up. Which meant the release of just kicking back in a chat room had become nearly impossible.

Release or escape, it was all the same thing.

That just left poor reception on a television that should've been replaced ten years ago, or curl up with a book on the deck. At least her father had taken care of that over the past few years. She'd spent more than a few evenings there, as long as she'd had the anti-mosquito candles lit. A good book, cup of coffee or wine cooler, and she could almost forget the real reason she'd returned home.

A new start, or a chance to find an old one she'd overlooked?

Gods, who was she kidding? A life here? With Victor or anyone else just wasn't going to be possible. Better she remember that and focus on getting back on her feet. She needed some money, the job she had committed to, and then a place to live where she could still have her privacy and hopefully a decent net connection.

She pulled up outside the cabin, leaning forward on the steering wheel, hands clenching as she replayed every moment in the diner with him.

Victor. Shit. Why had he walked into the diner like that? She'd got herself settled, had relaxed, and then he'd walked back into her life.

He'd not lost any of his looks. It would have been easier if he had.

Who was she trying to kid? Even if she ignored his looks, there was his voice, that low rumble behind his words, like a growl that fought to escape. His eyes, hazel, gold flecks, the warm knowing look deep within them; she could have looked into them for the rest of her life and been content.

Men like him didn't look at women like her. They chose cheerleaders, beauty queens, or business women who knew what they wanted and how they were going to get it. But not her type.

Would it be so wrong to be kissed by him just once?

Those soft lips, always the hint of a smile even when he was angry about something. She could almost feel it. A brush against her lips, the feel of his hand in her hair, tangling into the softness as his lips claimed hers. Heat, a wicked dampness, clenched through her core, and she pressed her thighs tightly together. Her nipples crinkled, brushing against her shirt, and a low moan vibrated from the back of her throat.

Would he hold her? His hands slide into her hair as he kissed her?

He'd growl, somehow she knew he'd growl in the moment before he kissed her. His teeth nipping at her lips, one hand firmly gripping her ass until she ...

She was acting like a teenager again. He wouldn't look her way, and even if he did, after what he'd said in the diner she'd sooner slap him than date him.

So why did her hips jolt at the thought of him?

Screw the coffee; she needed a hot shower.

Or better yet, a cold one.

Scars

* * * * *

Do you honestly think she'll give you the time of day after today?

"I'll just have to try extra hard, then," he muttered into the rearview mirror. "If I don't, Craig will corner her and force the issue, or another pack member will. I can't permit that to happen."

Ah, it's finally hit you, hasn't it?

He growled, clenched hands punching the steering wheel. As much as he didn't like to admit it, he didn't have a lot of choice now. If he didn't make a play for her, one of the others would, and they might not take no for an answer. Rape. The thought horrified him, but the pack was running out of time.

He couldn't sink that low. Not even if the pack was at stake. Could he?

Are you so confident you'll fail in seducing her? You're the alpha, the head of the pack, just as long as someone else doesn't decide to be rid of you. You've got a lot more in the way of resources at your fingertips than you've ever admitted to.

It was one thing to know about them, another to use them. "What if she doesn't want me?"

Doubt. Weird. He wasn't used to that emotion. Not when it came to women.

You smelt her, didn't you, or have you been spending too long in human form?

It hadn't been that long, two weeks or so, maybe closer to three since he'd shifted. Not that it mattered; the drive, the senses remained. Muted, but they were still there. It had been too long since he had shifted form and run through the forests at full pelt.

Deer. Hunting season was always open for his kind. Deer, rabbit, and occasionally another of his kind that stepped out of line.

You should have taken Craig out a long time ago. The ultimate

36

hunt, isn't it? Another shifter, another wolf. He weakens the pack.

"He probably says the same thing about me." He grunted, running his fingers through his hair. Damn stuff needed cutting again. "He might be right. If I'd done something before Simone left the area, we wouldn't be in this mess." Someone should have prevented her from leaving.

True, but it doesn't mean you should just give up and let him walk all over you. Yes, you should have stopped her from leaving and dealt with this problem years ago, but you can't live in the past. Now, get out there, talk to the female, use that charm on her. Are you an alpha, or a cub still needing his sire's protection?

That was uncalled for. He'd not needed his father's protection since his teenage years. Even then, he'd railed against the hovering shadow of the older man's image. Dark amber eyes, tawny hair, the sort of man that made women stop in their tracks, and yet most had never understood just why he'd been so devoted to the quiet woman at his side. Not when he could've had any woman he wanted, just by crooking his finger her way. He'd been a rare man and had missed so very little going on around him, especially when it concerned his son.

Craig had been behind the accident. Victor just hadn't been able to prove it. No one else in the pack would have dared such a cowardly act. Struck down from behind, not even faced off in a fight, or challenge. Craig, damn that man. One day Victor would get enough proof together.

What if it hadn't been a member of the pack?

No, Craig being responsible was the only thing that made sense.

Sneaky, though. Didn't even leave a trace of scent behind. You have to wonder how he managed that. Or are you just too willing to blame any problems on him? You and I both know it could easily have been some thug from the football game, or just some out of town yahoo. You've no proof. You just want to blame him because it fits with your view of the world.

Scars

"I don't wonder. I just want him dead, or at least gone. Dealt with," he muttered, knuckles turning white under the pressure. He could almost feel it, his fingers clenched about Craig's throat, the soft gurgle, pulse racing under his grip. So there had been no sign of the attacker before or since that night, but it didn't mean that Craig was blameless. "I'll find a reason to take him out at some point."

You don't need a reason. You're the alpha, leader of the pack; he's a member and isn't obeying you. He's trying to undermine your control. It's a very simple thing. You challenge him and take him out. Just think about it, how his blood will taste, the feel of his skin tearing beneath your teeth.

He didn't want to think about it, too tempting. Far better to focus on how he was going to approach Simone.

Well you could sit out here all day, staring at the cabin, or I don't know ... get out of the truck, walk up to her door, knock on it, and actually talk to the female. She won't bite you. The biting is your job.

Chapter Six

Hot water pounded against her body, beading on her skin. Steam curled upwards, caressing her form, sliding over damp flesh as soapy fingers left a slick coating on her bare skin. She needed this. After the day she had been through, the tension, all the stress, she needed this moment of sheer bliss under the shower. One thing she'd insisted on as a teenager had been the fitting of a decent shower in the cabin, and it had been the only argument where the cabin had been concerned that she'd won without a month or more of fights first.

No sign of her father, just a few scattered notes, phone calls she'd missed. A man who'd not left a name. Telesales, no doubt. They'd call back later if it was important. Who else could it have been?

Simone closed her eyes, letting the hot water pound against her face, small droplets pulling on taut nipples, washing off the soft suds as she gave herself to the hedonistic bliss of the moment.

Did he enjoy showers in the same way?

The thought caught her off guard, muscles tensing across her shoulders, her teeth grazing her bottom lip. What was she doing thinking about Victor?

Why not? He wasn't here; he'd never know, and her father was out with some old friends trying to empty one of the local lakes of fish. Or he was settled down with a few of his buddies, making plans for when deer season started?

Her fingers slid down over her breasts, cupping them, pinching softly at the peaks of her pink-tinged nipples, forcing a low moan into life. Her thighs pressed tightly together, hips rolling as she replayed his features in her mind. He'd kiss her ever so gently at first, then claim her lips, growling, fingers tight in her hair. Gods, she could feel it, the soft tip of his tongue prying into her mouth, seeking, stroking, his hands cupping her ass, pulling her tight against his muscled form.

So many women had dreamed of him, and she'd just be one of the hundreds that glanced his way. But she would never let him know. A secret to keep her warm through the nights ahead.

One hand eased down over her stomach, seeking between her thighs, cupping the soft mound of her sex with a gentle touch. Would he be tender? Or just take what he wanted. No, he'd show a mix of both. The strength wrapped in velvet desire.

With a low groan, her finger sought out her tight nub, brushing over the slick flesh, hips pressing taut against that wicked touch. Slow, tender, she tapped the tight little bud, soft gasps escaping parted lips, her hips rolling toward each light caress as it forced her into the realms of pleasure.

She leaned against the edge of the bath, one foot pressing onto the rim, thighs spread, her free hand grasping the railing as she found a way to balance under the steaming pleasure of the soft drumming beads of water. She groaned, sliding one finger into her clenching core, thumb replacing her finger against her slick clit. So good, wicked, wanton, delicious, a dozen words and more slipped through her mind, teasing her senses as she thrust her finger into her core, pressing it against the tight walls of her eager sex.

His lips, his touch, soft nibbling kisses, teeth grazing over her throat. Gods. She could almost smell him. Taste him.

More. Gods, she needed so much more.

Her hips rocked, and she groaned as her fingers played over her sensitive skin.

Water dripped from her nipples, tugging at them, pulling the way his fingers would. Soft patterns formed on her skin, dripping down, tender touches in a hundred places. So much pleasure, delight; she could see him, feel him pressed against her slick body, cupping her breasts, his cock pressing against her core, thrusting in, lifting her in the shower.

Just a few touches extra. Gods. Did he know how he fueled the dreams of the local women? Not something she would tell him; it would have only added to the natural arrogance that oozed from his being.

Her thighs tightened, a deeper rock pushing through her hips, teeth catching on her bottom lip as she growled, head leaning against the water-slick tiles, toes curling about the edge of the bath. Pressure built, controlled her thighs, her sex and her stomach. Ripples of pleasure, pain, and desire all melted into one, shuddering through her body in a low moan of release.

She shuddered, leaning against the shower walls for a moment, sweat washed from her body by the soothing warm water.

A sharp knock on the door dragged her out of the remnants of her release.

"Who's there?" Her toes found the faucet, turning the water off as she called out, snatching a towel from the railing.

"Victor."

Heat claimed her face, flushing over her body in an instant. "Hold on a few. I'll be right there." Had he heard her? She hoped not; the water should have masked what had been going on, or he might have assumed that she was just enjoying her time in the shower.

At least it wouldn't have been a lie, not really.

Still, to have to face him moments after he'd been the source of her fantasy was a situation right out of a bad dream. Or good dream if he ...

No, that thought needed to be stopped right there. Her jaw clenched, and she scrubbed the water from her body before she pulled on a robe, wrapped a towel about her hair, and headed for the front door. But try as she might, she couldn't quite push away the images of Victor, naked in the shower with her.

"Hello, I, erm ... did I disturb you?" He smiled as his gaze moved over her still damp form, lingering on the vee of skin at the

Scars

neck of her robe.

"Showering. I was just finishing off when you knocked."

"Sorry, I didn't mean to disturb you." He shifted a little on the deck, avoiding her gaze for a moment before he finally met her eyes. "I need to apologize for what I said to you back in the diner. I was out of line."

"It happens." She leaned against the edge of the door, not letting him in. The last thing she needed was him lingering in the living room with her dashing around her room trying to get dressed. "But you're one of the few that has ever had the guts to apologize to me for it. I shouldn't have brought up old rumors either. That was wrong of me. I've let myself fall into the habit of striking out first before others can lash out at me."

He shrugged, taking a step back before resting on the railing that surrounded the front deck. The day was drawing in, a soft pink and orange tinge filtering into the sky, the air cooler than it had been during the day and a warm breeze carrying with it the sound of the birds from the lake. Almost the sort of setting that would be better fitted to lovers making up than two who barely knew each other.

"I can understand that. Doesn't mean it was right, but you admitted it wasn't." His voice was soft, lacking the harsh tone that would have turned his words into an accusation.

"Thank you. You didn't have to come all the way out here to do this, though." Especially as it had come right on the tail end of her shower escapade.

"I didn't. Not just to apologize, though that was the main reason. I wanted to ... well, I'm going to a barbecue this evening, and I wondered if you'd like to come with me." He didn't glance away, no hints of it being a joke, or some cruel trick. How many of those had she lived through during high school?

Too many, but never from him.

"Why me?"

"Because I'd like to spend the time with you. We've not had

the chance to talk much over the years, and now that you're home I'd like to rectify that. If you don't mind?" He brushed back a stray lock of hair from his eyes, that familiar smile quirking the corners of his lips. "I'd like to learn a little more about you."

"Should I trust you?" Harsh question to ask, but she needed to know the answer. "After all the times you've sat back and listened to their words, just why should I trust you? For all I know, you could be setting me up."

"I could be, yes, but that's a risk you need to decide if you're willing to take. No matter what you might think of me, Simone, I've never knowingly set a woman up for a fall like that. I've dated a few, dumped them, but that was a long time ago. We've both changed." He parked his butt on the railing, grasping it as he settled down fully. "I know some of the boys at school could be pretty mean, but I'm not like that. I've never been like that."

She didn't speak for a moment, her gaze wandering openly over his form, lingering on the expanse of his chest. Did he still work on the land he had inherited from his father? Cutting wood, taking care of the land, looking after the house he now lived in alone, if she was guessing correctly.

What had happened to the old man?

Dead, she knew that much, just about the time she had left town. The rumors had been rife, everything from a drunken brawl to a hunting accident. She tried wracking her memories to recall just what the official story had been. Unlawful death by person or persons unknown.

Her gaze moved back to him as she tried to keep her thoughts straight.

A suntan, not the sort that came out of a box, or from hours spent under a lamp, but the natural sort that only came from working out in the fresh air. He'd gained a weathered look that softened the too perfect appearance of earlier years. His hands were rougher than she remembered, calloused, adding to the image of a man who worked hard for his living and wasn't ashamed of doing so.

"I guess I'm being a little harsh." She gave a small shrug.

"With good reason, but yes, you are."

"Damn, you don't pull punches, do you?" She blinked, then met his firm gaze.

"Why would I? Life's too short to dance around the truth."

"I guess it is." Too long in the city. Maybe she was being unfair, but so many there had said one thing whilst they were obviously thinking another. The blunt way of so many of her neighbors, even if the words had often been hurtful, had still been easier to deal with than the small smiles and murmured lies.

"So, will you come with me? To the barbecue?" He wasn't about to let the matter just drop.

"Where is it being held?"

"Ann's place, her mom. She asked me to attend, and I'd rather go with someone I want to spend time with instead of being open to her little hunting tactics."

A mercy date. All right, that made sense in some odd way. For a moment she hesitated, ready to tell him no, that he could take his pity elsewhere, until she saw the look in his eyes. A soft light, tender smile that beckoned to her. If anyone was asking for a mercy date it was him, not her being offered one. He needed her. For the first time someone actually needed her. If only to keep Ann at arm's length.

"I'd love to. Just give me a little time to get ready, will you?"

"I'll be right here on the deck, if that's okay with you?"

Simone smiled, relaxing under the warmth in his gaze. "Yes, yes, of course. I won't be long."

Just as long as it took her to find something to wear. Somehow turning up to a barbecue in a robe and towel didn't seem like the best of ideas, no matter how much she wanted to rub Ann's nose in it.

Chapter Seven

She'd actually said yes. After everything he'd said to her, not just in the diner but during those long foolish days of youth, she had actually agreed to go to the party with him.

I never doubted she would. She likes you.

Like had nothing to do with it. After the diner, she'd have had every right to slap him and then slam the door in his face. Even recovering from the shower the way she'd claimed, she'd remained a strange mix of calm and excited. Odd that, for someone who'd just been cleaning off, she'd smelt almost aroused.

Maybe she was. Some have been known to combine water and pleasure before. I hear it can be quite interesting. You should try it. Perhaps with Simone?

Not something he could ask her about, not even when he caught a glimpse of the sweet upper curves of her breasts in the parting of her robe. Did she have any idea what she did to him? He groaned inwardly, tugging his jeans back down over the hardening line of his erection. The thought of her body wet, willing and able beneath the soft caress of water from above only added to the sweet ache that throbbed through his body.

His mate.

Or she would be if only he didn't screw things up with her. If she didn't want him, then he'd find a way to protect her from the dangers that lingered at the edge of his world. Even if it meant showing her those dangers firsthand.

Sweet hips, soft lips, the way her eyes pierced into his soul to seek answers. The hurt she'd been through over the years was palpable, an open wound he couldn't ignore. That only added to the growing drive he fought, the need to protect her, claim her, keep her from harm and the stalking dangers of others.

Craig.

Scars

His teeth clenched. The man would be there tonight. In taking Simone, he opened her up to danger. He knew that, but he couldn't keep avoiding bringing her out into the public with him, staking some sort of limited claim on the woman. Even if she didn't know he was doing that.

Craig would have known by now; the entire pack would be on the lookout for her. Even the other male members of the pack would be hopeful that they could take advantage of this delicious-looking female with the potential to save them all.

You can't hide it from her for much longer. One of the other pack members will catch on. If not Craig then Jim, or Steve. They all are going to sense her return sooner or later, if they haven't already. Most will wait to see you make a move, but they won't wait too much longer. Not with what's at risk. Not one single newcomer can be brought into the pack and no half-blood or turned female until you choose your mate.

Until the pack alpha did.

Ann wouldn't be impressed by his actions. The man she wanted, a fact half the town was aware of, bringing Simone to the party would be a public slap in Ann's face. Good, she needed it. The woman had been stalking him for too long, always lingering on the edge of his life. That was exactly why Craig had bedded her and now continued to do so. He'd marked the woman with his scent, knowing that if Victor ever gave in to the need to sate his lust with Ann, he'd do so with the full knowledge that he was using the castoff from a lesser member of the pack.

Mind games, power plays and struggles to keep each other off balance until the time was right for them to face off. Sometimes he wanted to walk away from the whole mess. Not a choice he really had.

"Ready?" She slipped out of the door, a soft summer dress whispering around her thighs. Straps that left her shoulders and neck bare, a light yellow cotton, sweet curves that covered her breasts but left enough of their swell exposed to his gaze. Dark hair long and loose down her back fell in soft curls still semi-damp from the shower.

She filled his senses, consuming him.

"Yes, very." He struggled to keep the low growl from his voice. It would have been so very easy to step forward, pull her into his arms, and taste her. How could he go through with this, without claiming her, feeling her body arch beneath his in a soft, delicious bow of delight? "Did you want to ride with me, or follow me in your own car?"

She glanced toward the truck she used, then back at him. "Is there a reason I'll want to leave without you?"

"I hope not."

"Then I'll ride with you."

Good, at least she trusted him that far. He'd have to keep that trust, fight to control his instincts, the drive to reach for her, pull her tight against him, nibble his way down her throat, across that throbbing pulse point. "Glad to hear that. I'm hoping we'll get the chance to catch up on what you've been doing since you left home."

She flowed past him in a cloud of thin yellow cotton. He could almost see through it in places, the darker points of her nipples, the light covering of barely there panties. Even with the clean clothing, he could smell it, the soft, musky scent of arousal. Just her smell, no man, perfume, or anything else to taint the scent that beckoned the beast lurking within his skin. "You already know that. I told you when we were in the diner."

"Kyle. Yes, you mentioned him, but nothing of you, your work, what you'd been doing."

"Other than staying out of the way of his bad moods, there's not been a lot of time for anything else in all honesty. Kyle had this way of working himself into every aspect of my life, controlling it, destroying it if I found one moment of happiness without him. Except for Mandy. She and I had coffee on a regular basis. We talked, and I went through a dozen part-time jobs. Kyle didn't like me working; it gave me far too much in the way of independence." Simone glanced back at him.

He closed the door behind her and got in from the other side. Long enough to work out how he was going to approach this and try to regain some measure of control. "But you still managed to get enough money together to make it home?"

"He was working full time, for a while, and that let me get a little work in. Decent money, office temp. Turned out the skills I'd picked up with computers were worth something after all."

"Skills?"

"I spent a lot of time, before I found some work to keep me busy, playing around on my computer. A form of company, I guess. It didn't pay to step outside at times."

No doubt it hadn't. Not with some of the bruises she might have been sporting. "Well, I'm glad you managed to make some good out of it all."

She nodded, falling into silence, her gaze drifting out toward the window. She'd been through too much, more than most would ever have wanted to know about. It would take time, and a level of trust that as yet didn't exist between them.

"Ann won't be happy to see you there."

"I know," she murmured.

"Is that why you accepted the invitation?"

"No, I had other reasons, though I wonder if they were wise now." A soft tremor touched her words.

"You've nothing to fear from me."

"Ann is another matter. She'd tip me in the lake at the first chance. Good job I can swim." A twitch of full lips brought the shadow of a true smile and the hint of a humor she normally buried. "I might be forced to drag her in after me, of course, but then I doubt you or any of the other men at the party will object to a mud fight."

Mud, her soft skin, the cotton clinging to her form, outlining her breasts, hard nipples, molding to the smooth outline of her mound. He fought back a groan. "No, I can't see anyone objecting to that."

"You'd watch?"

"Yes. I'm a man, but I'm not completely stupid. The two don't always go hand in hand."

She chuckled, light touching her eyes, a weight lifting visibly from her slender shoulders. "Some would disagree."

Chapter Eight

She was flirting with him, openly flirting with him. What had gotten into her? It wouldn't do any good. He was doing this to send a clear signal to Ann, and maybe try and make amends with her for this afternoon.

No, a man like him could never truly be interested in someone like her.

So why did he look at her so intently? His gaze lingered on her breasts, moved over her body with an open admiration. Foolish, he didn't want to take things further than a date, or two, maybe a brief kiss. The first time he touched the scars he'd draw back, they all did.

Her nipples hardened, thighs clenching tight, a soft warmth rippling within her core. Her lips tingled, parting, wanting to feel his touch, his tongue tracing deep inside her mouth, offering her his passion the same way she craved to give him hers in return.

"When did she ask you to the party?"

"Just after you two had gone at it in the middle of the street."

"So you really are trying to prove a point to her?" Is that what it boiled down to, him sticking it to Ann? Gods, please don't let it be just that? Even if it was, would it be so bad?

Yes. No. Damn how was she expected to know that before taking the plunge and going through with the party?

"It's more than that." He glanced back at her, pulling off the road long before they reached the outskirts of Ann's property. "We've got a little time, and I do need to talk to you. The trouble is, this is going to sound like a set of lines, and I don't want that."

She frowned, watching him closely, mentally taking note of where they were going. The picnic area. It should be safe enough. Tourists often used the place; it was well traveled and not the sort of area that screamed warnings of date rape. This time of day, the local police did a drive-by, if she was remembering it correctly.

Date rape wasn't his style. What had gotten into her?

Not him that was the problem.

Her thighs clenched beneath her dress, a wave of heat coating her inner walls. Her breath caught at the back of her throat, the thought of his touch tracing a slow, teasing path along her inner thigh ...

Gods, she had to get that image out of her mind.

"Something the matter? You look a little uncomfortable. I don't blame you." The truck stopped on the edge of the parking lot, wooden benches and tables in easy view. "I guess this does seem a little odd for you. For me also."

"What's going on?" She turned in the seat, looking closely at him. What did he need to discuss with her that left him feeling odd?

Oh, gods. What if he was about to say he was gay and the whole ego thing, everything in a skirt during high school, had been nothing more than a really good cover?

"I want more than one date with you, Simone. I'd like to get to know you, to spend a lot of time with you, maybe date ..."

"You want to date me?" Shock dried out her throat. All those years of watching him had paid off. Would finding out he really was gay have been easier to cope with? No. This had to be a bad joke. Her heart dropped into the pit of her stomach. A trap. She'd walked right into it in the dumb hope he might actually like her. She turned in the seat, searching for the telltale signs that she was being set up. "Where's the camera, the video? You're setting me up, aren't you?"

"No, I swear. It's nothing like that. What do I have to do to get you to see that I like you?" He groaned, banging his head back against the padded headrest. "Okay, that was badly phrased. What is it? I've been told that I could charm the birds from the sky, have a dozen women eating out of my hands with a few well-placed words if I actually wanted that. Not that I believe that, or want that ... I'm not making any sense, am I? I guess I'm trying to say that normally I feel at ease around women, comfortable even ... but put me in the same area as you, and I turn into an idiot stammering for the right thing to say."

"Have you been drinking?" She hadn't smelt it on him, but he was acting almost drunk.

"No, though I wish I had been; it would make it so much easier. I'd have an excuse for acting like a complete fool." Strong fingers rubbed at his temples. "I can't get this straight, not without making an even bigger idiot of myself than I already have."

"Just come out and say it." She edged closer, fighting the temptation to touch his arm. She was imagining things, of course. He was playing a game. He had to be.

"I'm asking you to be my ma-- my girlfriend."

"You almost said something else there." His ma--? She struggled to find the rest of the missing word.

"A word best left unsaid for now," he sounded older, from another time and place with how he phrased things. An old soul wrapped in a younger body.

"And why should I believe you? Why would you want to go out with me for more than a single night?" The tension, she could see it, nearly taste it as it played across his shoulders. Something left unsaid.

"I need you," a throaty growl. "It's that simple. I need you, in ways I don't have the words to explain. You're in my blood, my thoughts."

Common sense said back away, get out of the truck, and make a break for it, but the look in his eyes, such a hunger, something she had never seen before, at least not directed at her. Words that should have been kept locked away until the end of her days gained life as she watched every move he made. "Show me what you mean."

He didn't move, not at first, shock registering across his face, a light, a hope touching his gaze, turning the golden flecks into a soft warm glow.

"Are you sure?" His words where little more than a whisper.

"Yes." She didn't move. If this was a mistake, then let it be one she could at least enjoy.

A low, soft growl formed at the back of his throat as he reached for her, his hands tangled into her hair, pulling her close against him. Lips parted, a kiss softer than she had ever imagined brushed hers. Gentle, possessive, and loving. Words she'd never thought to associate with him, yet they now purred through her thoughts.

She whimpered, her lips parting beneath his, suckling on his tongue as it slid into her mouth, stroking, exploring every inch of her warmth. The grip in her hair tightened, then relaxed, still holding her in place as he edged closer to her, leaning in across the cab of the truck.

No wandering hands, no groping, or attempts to shed her of clothing, just a long deep kiss that rocked through her body.

Tenderly he pulled back from the kiss, his hands easing from her hair, strong fingers massaging her neck, his voice a soft, low whisper. "That's what I mean. I need you the same way I need air. Does it make sense? No, of course not, but I can't deny it. I'm not asking you to marry me, or agree to spend the rest of your life with me. Not yet, at least. But accept one thing as the truth. I need you, Simone. I always have."

Always? A single word yet it held more power than she had ever imagined possible.

She wanted to believe him. She almost needed to fall into his words and let them wrap around her the same way the warmth of his kiss now burned within her core. Her lips were on fire with the need to feel his pressed to her once more. A throbbing, wicked need worked through her hips, soft jolts threatening to take control of her body.

Would it be so wrong, just to believe him, to accept what he offered?

He wasn't lying. Somehow she knew that. No lie would have

Scars

left him shifting like a school boy waiting to hear her response.

His touch, she could still feel his touch. Her skin tingled, craving so much more than the brief caress he had given her. Promises of so much more lay hidden beneath that kiss and behind his words.

She wanted him, needed him.

Yes. She could say yes. It wouldn't have taken that much. A single word and the dream would begin.

Dreams were dangerous. She'd learned that the hard way.

A low tremble ran through her body, her lips parting as she gave life to the words that cut through her heart.

"I can't."

Chapter Nine

"What do -- do you mean you can't? Tha-- that doesn't make any sense. I don't understand." Had he misunderstood her?

"Exactly that, I just can't. I'll go with you to the party tonight, spend some time with you, but I can't believe that you actually need me." She hesitated for a moment. "It was very sweet of you to say that. Don't get me wrong. I'm flattered, but I just don't believe you. After all the lies I swallowed from Kyle, I'm just not prepared to enter another relationship, even one that starts out as dating, if it's based on a lie."

His breath caught in the back of his throat, panic surging into life. She'd refused him? This couldn't be happening. Women didn't refuse him, not like this and not when he wanted them.

But it is happening. Odd that. Things were going so well. I guess you'll just have to shift, bite her, then persuade her later that it was for her own good. Of course, you're not sure what's going on. Honestly speaking, she might not be aware of just how fortunate she is, being chosen by you instead of one of the others.

What? He had to be kidding. Just bite her and force the issue? Didn't the wolf spirit understand that it was akin to rape?

Is that such a hard thing to imagine doing? It's what our kind does. We choose our mates, take them off, bite them, and help bring them over. Most of them don't even mind after it takes place. It's a very simple process.

"I do need you, more than you can ever understand." Not unless he did exactly what the wolf guide told him to do. "I wish I could get you to understand that."

"Why do you? You just said you need me. No reasons, no explanations, just the need." Simone gave a soft shake of her head.

"You'd never believe me." He shook his head, trying to shake away the voices of doubt. "I want to be able to tell you, but you'd look at me as if I was nuts. Maybe I am. God knows, I feel like I am, half the time." His fingers pressed against his temples, rubbing softly.

Mates. The need. Her refusal. No wonder his head hurt.

You're not nuts. You're a werewolf, a shifter, the alpha of your pack if you live long enough to claim the position fully, complete with a mate. Not sure what will happen if you don't claim her. Though you could try and show her the meaning of it all. The why behind the need.

Show her the pack?

No, not the pack, just himself. The real deal. Everything that becoming involved with him would entail.

And send her screaming into the night in the process. Wonderful.

What if it backfired on him and she ended up revealing the existence of werewolves to everyone else?

And just who do you think would believe her?

That part wasn't such a huge problem. The wolf spirit had a point. Werewolves, shifters, the tree spirits and guardians, the whole package of magical or cursed beings was nothing more than a myth that the rest of the world gleefully ignored. Even when they were faced with the reality of such beings.

So what have you got to lose?

Good question.

His sanity, well that was long gone. His pride, a fragile commodity at best and easy to rebuild. His status with Simone? That didn't exist, not truly.

Not yet at least.

"Try me." Simone's eyes narrowed.

Had she been able to follow the line of thought that he had been struggling with?

He shook his head, trying to fight back the growing uncertainty, the drive to change into his other form if for no other reason than to show her what was going on. "My father fell in love with my mother many years before they actually married. He needed her and fought it, not wanting to give into the drive, but from the day they met he knew the answer. It wasn't something he could ignore."

"A family trait?" One delicate eyebrow arched.

"In more ways than one. I wish I could show you, explain it to you, but you'd never believe me." Who would without deciding they were insane?

"Never is a very long time."

She has you there. It's far longer than you could ever imagine.

Blasted wolf.

I'm right. You know it.

"Okay, just ... we'll head to the barbecue, and if you still want to know what I'm talking about after that, I'll show you. I promise." At least by then it would be dark; he'd be able to shift without the risk of being seen so easily. He'd have to pick a quiet place to do it, though, away from the town, and the others in the pack.

The last thing he needed was Craig or one of the others stumbling in on his little version of show and tell.

"After the party? Okay, I'm going to hold you to that."

Of that he had no doubt.

Chapter Ten

Was she mad, insane, out of her mind? She had to be. How long had she waited for him to hold her like that, kiss her, and now she was turning him down. Gods, what had gotten into her? Her lips tingled from the kiss, ached to be touched again; her body felt alive in a way she had never known before, yet she'd turned him down until he could explain what was going on.

Insane. Completely and utterly insane.

What had she done?

Refused him based on what? A whim? On thinking he would turn out just like Kyle? No, Kyle would have become angry, fought, lashed out either with words or his fists. Not Victor. He'd tried to reason with her instead.

Rare. Beautiful. So very strong in ways she had never imagined.

Neither of them spoke now as he turned the truck around and back toward the road. The barbecue, time with some of the others she'd grown up with and a little distance between them might give her mind the chance to clear.

Clear from what?

His touch, the low musky scent that lingered around him, the way he affected every inch of her body without a single touch.

She glanced over at him, but said nothing. Neither of them had anything to say, despite the tension that had settled over them both. There were too many questions and no real answers.

Not until after the party, or so it seemed.

Gravel crunched under the tires, the truck turning off from the main road and down the small track. Ann's place had once been a farmstead, but the farmhouse had been demolished years ago. A modern, sprawling home had taken its place. Money, and too much of it, had been poured into making the house look like something that would have been better suited to a luxury housing estate.

Show-offs, that was the polite term for Ann's family. Snobs, the rich jet set. There were truly cruel names she could have applied to Ann's people, but after some of the things she'd been called, Simone wasn't likely to fall into that trap.

"She's going to freak, you know that?" He pulled up in front of the house, turning the engine off. "If you want to back out, I'd understand. I'll take you home if you decide that's what you need to do."

"Ann? Yes, I guess she is." Freak was one word for it; she'd throw a fit in more ways than one, but not until she had the chance to go somewhere private, unless she was given the chance to throw a fit publicly in a way that would benefit her. "No, I'm fine. I've no intention of backing out. After all, you've promised to do a little show and tell for me later. Unless you've changed your mind."

"Well, then, we'll have to wait and see what she does." He flashed a grin her way, stepping out of the truck. There he waited long enough for her to walk around the side of the truck to meet up with him. "I meant what I said earlier. I'll explain things after the party, if you give me the chance to."

She believed him. She had to. If he was lying then she didn't know what she'd do. Or how she'd handle the simmering emotions she now struggled to bury deep within. "I know when the party is over." She nodded, looking around at the dozens of cars. "Are you sure this is just a barbecue? Looks as though half the business owners in the area are here."

Cars better suited for cities and freeways lined the gravel-covered driveway. A few decent trucks and SUVs, but for the most part the sort of vehicles that didn't belong on gravel paths. "I get the feeling Ann wasn't being entirely truthful about the situation."

"It wouldn't be the first time." Annoyance tinged his words, a frown deepening across his brow. "We could just leave, but I'm pretty sure we've already been seen."

Scars

Simone glanced around, catching sight of a group of people at the side of the house. "And they'd have already told Ann or others about you being here, so we might as well put on a good show for them, unless you don't want to leave Ann choking on her own anger."

"Oh, I think I can be persuaded to do that." He smiled, relaxing as he slid his arm through hers. "So I suggest we go and find the hostess and her daughter, then see how long it takes for Ann to break into a coughing fit."

An hour, no more than that, and she'd get to the bottom of it with him, all being well.

"Victor? I wasn't expecting you to bring someone with you." Ann moved through the gathered men and women, a glass of wine in each hand. "Oh, Simone ..."

"Well, I thought this would be a good chance for Simone to catch up with some old friends." He pulled her closer, settling one arm about her waist. "You don't mind, do you?"

She leaned into his touch, partly for show. But only partly. It felt right. Being in his arms like that.

Just a good show they were putting on for the woman whose gaze narrowed on them. No, it was more than that. Victor had made that clear. Explanations would be when the time was right, when he could show her just what was going on. Or whatever it was he had planned. Until then, she planned on trying to enjoy being with him.

His date.

Ann's gaze darkened, her jaw tight, the glasses shaking in her hands. "No, why would I?"

"Glad to hear that, I wouldn't want to cause any trouble." Victor smiled, brushing the back of his fingers against Simone's cheek. That soft, tender touch that left her wanting more. She had to keep that under control, fight it and keep the urges he had brought to life from taking over.

It would have been so easy to lean into him, turn to face him, her lips parted with the need to feel his kiss once more.

"Victor, good to see you again."

He tensed, fingers digging into her side. "Hello, Craig."

Craig. Why did she know that name? She peered around Victor, looking over the other man. With blue eyes, dark brown hair that had been touched by the sun, he had the same sense of power that Victor had, a body well formed by work outside the house. Farm work, land work, it didn't matter. He showed signs of that same honest labor. Only with Craig something else lay beneath it.

Arrogance. Not the self-assurance she'd seen in Victor, but sheer arrogance that left her skin crawling under the path of his blatant gaze.

"And this must be Simone. It's been a while." His gaze moved over her body in the same way Victor's had. No, not entirely true. Not the same way. Close. Something lay hidden beneath that assessment.

Something hungry.

"Perhaps Craig could keep Simone company whilst you and I go for a walk, Victor?" Ann suggested, a smile settling on her perfectly painted lips. "We do have a lot to catch up on, and I know my mom was looking to discuss a little business with you. You still do some landscaping work from time to time, don't you?"

"I thought this was a party." Victor scowled and shook his head. "Not a chance to pick up some extra work."

"It is, but you wouldn't deny the hostess the chance to talk to you now that you're here, would you?" Ann smiled, setting the glasses down on a nearby table. "Please, just for a short while. Simone will be perfectly safe; Craig will look after her, won't you, Craig?"

No. Ann didn't have the right to separate them like this. She wasn't a piece of meat to be passed from one man to another.

"Of course, she'll be safe with me, Victor. You know that better than anyone else." Craig glided forward, easing Victor out of his

Scars

place, almost pushing the man toward Ann. "Now off you go. I'll take good care of her. I promise."

Her stomach knotted. The hunger she'd seen in Craig's eyes doubled, and there was nothing she could do about it from the way Ann now slid her arm through Victor's. That single move had blocked her chance to escape to the safety of Victor's side.

He'd come back. He had to. He wouldn't just leave her there with this Craig. Would he?

Chapter Eleven

Good care of her -- he'd eat her up the first chance he had.

So stay with her then. Don't let Craig and that damn female split you up. To hell with human manners. You don't have to play by their rules.

He did if he wanted to be able to conduct any business in the town, or keep the pack hidden. Some of the medical bills they incurred, the wounds, money would always be needed to take care of that side of things, and that meant working. Damn Craig, he knew that better than any other member of the pack. The alpha had to take care of the rest of the pack, cubs and adults alike.

"All right. Just for a short time, though." He nodded toward Ann, giving Craig a harsh look. "Don't move, because I won't be long, Simone."

Not a good idea. Still it's a party, you should be safe enough. Unless he finds a way to pull her away, take her out of sight. He might try that, you know. Craig isn't stupid.

His kind seldom were.

Simone wasn't going to back down to him like that. She'd stay where he'd told her, wouldn't she? Yes, of that he was certain. Still he glanced back again, offering her a smile and nodding to the deck where she now stood with Craig. "I won't be long, I promise."

"I know," Simone smiled, though she looked nervously at Craig if only for a moment. Did she sense the danger Craig presented?

She's a smart one. Isn't sure what's going on, but she's aware of how he is looking at her.

Sure she was, but he couldn't smell fear on her; neither could he smell desire, which was at least one good thing. If Craig had triggered a sense of arousal in Simone, he wouldn't have dared to leave her alone with his rival.

"Now, my mom has a lot she wants to talk to you about. She

might be a while, though. Are you sure you want to make the poor girl wait for you here when she could be more comfortable out by the lake, or in the den?" Ann slid one arm through his, turning him away from the rest of the group. "We should get a drink, a beer or wine, seeing as we're already mixing business with pleasure, don't you think?"

Pleasure, the word purred from her lips, a soft sound, sultry, hinting at the delights she sought from him.

She has a one-track bloody mind that female. Doesn't she ever go out of heat?

If he'd been drinking at the time he'd have lost it in a fit of coughing.

You know I'm right. All she ever thinks about is who she can mate with next. It's a good thing she hasn't produced any pups. I swear she'd be able to repopulate the entire pack herself, not to mention half the country, if she could litter the way true bitches do.

Not many of their kind were able to do that. A rare female would come along that shifted into wolf form and gave birth to a litter, only to return to human form a little later. But the last one Victor had heard about had died over a hundred years ago.

Would Simone have the capability to do that?

Oh, you'll find that out later.

"Now, just why did you have to bring that horrible creature with you? Was it pity?" Ann frowned. "You didn't have to bring someone with you, if all you could come up with was that thing."

"Creature?" He bristled, turning his attention fully toward Ann. "If you mean Simone, I suggest you remember she did come here as my date."

"Oh, please, everyone here knows you wouldn't really date a woman who looks like that. I mean, you could have any woman you wanted locally. Why would you pick someone who looks like that?" Safe in her own home, Ann showed no signs of holding back with her comments, a cold, cruel smile shining from the depths of her heartless eyes. "Have you taken a good look at her face? Those horrible scars. I don't know how she can live with herself."

He opened his mouth to speak only to close it again. Gods. What did he say to this?

"You're making a fool of yourself, Victor." Ann traced one finger lightly over his arm. "She's a loser; she'll always be a loser. Women like that would put out for anyone, but I doubt she gets it even if she offered money to the men in question. What were you thinking about, bringing her to the party? Oh, I understand. A mercy date, or you want something from her. Not sex, obviously, but something else."

He hesitated only long enough to keep his anger from taking control of his voice. His hands clenched tight at his sides, pulling free of her unwanted touch until he was able to turn and look her fully in the face.

"I don't care what you think of Simone. To me she's beautiful, strong, and honest. She's the sort of woman I could happily spend the rest of my life with if she would look my way, which she hasn't. Yet. So keep your goddamn evil mouth away from her. I won't stand here and let you tear into her again. She's done nothing to deserve that from you or anyone else."

If Ann had been a man, words wouldn't have entered the equation. A few swift punches, and it would have been over and done with. But with a woman ... No, he wasn't the type to strike them without a damn good reason.

"You think that now, but once she's spread her legs for you and you've scratched that itch, you'll be looking for something a little more interesting. A woman who knows how to please you and won't be treated like a freak by the local good old boys in the diner. You know what they call her -- witch, scar face, the freakoid. And those are the nicer comments." Ann didn't step back, her hands settled on her hips. "So think about it, Vic. You can waste your time with the hag, or you can finally make the right choice when it comes to women."

His throat tightened, a heavy coal burning in the pit of his stomach. "You'd best get one thing straight, Ann -- you will never be worth the time of day in my book. If you think I want Craig's castoff instead of the woman I've loved since high school, then you're out of your damn mind. If you have a mind left after the way you've fucked a path through the men of this town."

"You bastard, how dare you!"

"Oh, I'll dare a whole lot more if you ever turn your evil little tongue Simone's way again. Put it to better use, like wrapping it around whatever walking cock you're currently spending time with. Which would be Craig, if I'm not mistaken."

"I ..."

"Don't you dare accuse Simone of sleeping around when you're one of the biggest sluts I've ever had the misfortune of running into."

Even with his wolf-assisted senses, he never saw the slap coming.

Chapter Twelve

"I thought he'd never leave." Craig smiled, turning his attention fully on her. "Well, now, what brought you home after all these years?"

"It was just the right time to return." She stepped away from him, hoping to keep at least a few paces between them. The man set her nerves on edge, the hair on the back of her neck rising until she shuddered. He was older than both of them by five or six years at least, yet he still mixed with the same groups as Ann and her friends. Not something she'd ever been comfortable with. "I hadn't seen my father in some time."

"And is that the only reason?" His eyes flashed for a moment, tracing the line of her dress, lingering on her breasts. His gaze left her skin crawling. She might as well have been naked with the way he looked at her.

"Does it matter?" Why hadn't she grabbed a sweater to wear with this dress? Not that it would have helped right now.

"No, I don't suppose it does."

Why did he have to look at her like that? Did she have something on her face? Or had she found some new perfume that drew all the men to her? Not that she minded the attention from Victor, and in some small way she was actually flattered by the attention Craig was now paying her, as well. She just had the oddest feeling she was missing something in all this. "You've been busy, I guess, taking over your family business?"

"Sold it. Wasn't my thing." He shrugged, dismissing the subject as he took a step closer. "Can you see me manning some little shop for the rest of my life?"

"No, I don't suppose I can." She backed up, feeling the railing of the deck behind her. Dammit, nowhere left to go; she could dart to the other side, but it would've drawn too much attention her way. Not only that, but what reason did she have to run, except for feelings?

"Why did you come with Victor, of all people? Ann will be about ready to tear his throat out for this. You know she has a real interest in him, don't you?"

"It seemed like a good idea." At the time at least. How often had she mocked people for jumping into bad situations, only to do the same thing herself? "I needed a break from the city, too much noise, more people than I wanted to be around. And the party -- well, how better to get to know everyone again?"

Okay, she almost believed that herself. For three seconds at least.

He nodded, not speaking for a moment. "I'd like to get to know you again. I missed that opportunity before you left. Not a mistake I want to make again."

"Is there something going on?"

"What do you mean?" His eyes narrowed, jaw tense. All right, there was something. Now, if she could just find out what, everything would be fine and she could get on with her life.

Right?

"You and Victor, there's something going on. You both want to get to know me now? Have I come into some money that I haven't been told about yet? Or some other form of wealth?" That had to be the reason, two of the most sought after men in town and both of them pulling the same *I'd like to get to know you* line in the matter of a day.

"No, it's nothing like that." Color drained from his face. "You're well ... I mean ..."

"It's a game, between the two of you, to see who can get me in the sack first, isn't it?" Men, they were all alike, just wanting to find a way between your legs. Better yet, beat a friend to it, or a rival. Foolish to think Victor actually wanted her for herself and not some damn bet. "Well, it's not going to work. I'm not like that."

Maybe she was, but not in the way he obviously thought. Kyle had taught her too much about hasty mistakes. It didn't mean she wasn't about to think about men.

Men? Not just one man.

Oh no, she wasn't going down that line of thought. Not right now anyway.

Two warm bodies, one on either side of her. Two sets of lips brushing over the back of her neck, her breasts, her stomach …

Her thighs tightened, heat rippling through her core.

Gods, this wasn't the time or the place for this.

"It's not like that, not in the way you think." Craig whispered, cupping her cheek in one hand. "You're the key, you don't know what's going on, but I can tell you this, you're the key to it all for him, for me, and others."

Key? What the hell was he talking about? "You're drunk."

"I haven't touched a drop, seldom do. Don't like the way it smells."

Victor hadn't touched the wine or beer he'd been offered either, both men turning it down without a thought. "I don't remember ever seeing you take a drink."

"I did once, left me feeling ill for days, disorientated. Not something I'll do again." He spoke calmly, stroking her cheek, his gaze meeting hers without a hint of concern. "And you are more important that you could ever know."

He was touching the scars. Without drawing back, without cold remarks, he didn't flinch as he traced the lines that marked her face. Instead, his gentle touch continued. Men didn't touch her scars, not like this. It should have been a moment that she enjoyed, a time where her face didn't cause a look of revulsion, but she couldn't shake the ill-seated feeling that had settled in her core.

"Don't touch me, please." She tried to take a step back from him.

"I want to, not just like this but so much more." He leaned closer, brushing his lips across her throat, a hint of teeth scraping

Scars

her skin.

She whimpered, clenching her hands tight at her sides, a soft shudder working through her body. Despite everything, the discomfort she felt, his touch commanded her attention. Nipples hardened beneath the soft cloth, a tremor of need throbbing through her core, the soft jolt her hips couldn't deny. No. She didn't need this.

She wanted it though. Craig. Victor. What power did they have over her?

"Please don't," a murmured protest when she should have been screaming the word no instead.

"Why, you want it, you enjoy it; I can see it, feel it." He leaned closer, his breath caressing her ear. "Smell it."

Smell it? He couldn't. He didn't arouse her desires the same way Victor had. Though now she felt his breath, his touch, she couldn't ignore the tight rippling and heat that gathered between her thighs.

"Don't you want to explore it?" His lips brushed over hers, the whisper of a kiss that left her wanting more. His smell reminded her of something, a mix of musk, wood, grass, the scent of a forest just after the storm, not an artificial aftershave, or the harsh smell of alcohol. "The desire you feel sparking into life between us."

"I can't."

"Why not?" He didn't move back, every breath touched her face, his chest rising and falling, touching her breasts with each new drawing into his lungs.

"It's wrong. I'm here with Victor."

"Forget him. I can show you so much, take you into the depths of pleasure that you've never dreamed of. He can only claim you, take you, then toss you aside once you've served your purpose with him." A rumble in his voice, the hint of an animalistic growl that he barely kept under wraps.

"Purpose?" The promise Victor had given her, the explanation she needed.

"Something that you don't need to worry about beyond the knowledge that we need you. Either him, me, or another like us. It's your choice, to a degree. But eventually you'll have to pick one of us."

She bit back a cry, anger replacing discomfort. Every fiber of her being screamed out to strike, hit him across the face, send him stumbling back from her. So when the sound of hand on skin sounded, out it took a moment before she realized it hadn't come from something she'd done.

Chapter Thirteen

"You bastard, how dare you!" Ann's gaze narrowed and her jaw clenched. "How dare you treat me like this at my own party? Get out, get out now! I don't want to even look at you."

The growl left his lips before he had the chance to stop it, hands curling into claws, the wildness bubbling up from his soul. She'd struck him. Him. The alpha, the leader. A mere female had struck him just because he wouldn't fuck her.

Stupid little bitch. Just who did she think she was?

The hostess of a party. A woman he had just insulted.

Well, he'd had good reason. She'd lashed out without care toward Simone. As if it didn't matter that such words had plagued Simone through her life. Or that his date didn't deserve to be the target of attacks like that.

She was a woman whose beauty shone within her eyes; her grace and strength called to him with every breath. Yet to Ann she was nothing more than an invitation for mockery.

It went beyond that.

The physical blow was the final straw, the last insult to him and his family, his mate, that he was willing to take from the woman who stood in front of him.

"Hit me again, and I'll do a damn sight more than that." Snarled words, flecks of spit covered his lips; the drive to push her to the floor, pin her there, his teeth about her throat to teach her what her rightful position was in life. Beneath him, less than him.

Bad enough that he could half see Craig and Simone from the corner of his eye, closer than he was comfortable with, but this went too far.

"Are -- are you threatening me?" Ann took a half-step back from him. "I've never seen you like this. You're almost beast-like. Are you drunk, or high? I've never seen you like this. I want you out of here. Now. I won't be threatened by you or anyone else."

"No, I'm warning you." He growled, turning away from her without another word. If he stayed, the beast would be free; it would feed and tear her throat out without a single thought.

The animal side of his nature, the wolf defending itself from her attack, clawed at the edges of his sanity, demanding retribution. Blow for blow. A show of dominance that would teach the silly female a lesson she would never forget.

No, even in this mood you wouldn't attack her in such a manner. You'd think about it, close your jaws about her throat, but the drive to kill her isn't there. I know you, better than you are willing to admit.

She'd hit him, and deserved everything that he wanted to give her.

Would you turn yourself into Craig or this Kyle your female ran from? Right in front of her eyes, would you really become the walking nightmare?

He stiffened, cold hands clawing into his stomach, leaving lines of pain in their wake. Of all the things he could have been told that struck him the deepest. Men, real men, didn't abuse women. Especially ones they cared for, or loved.

And he loved Simone.

He couldn't let her see him like this. Not so close to being out of control. She'd run. And with good reason. He'd lose the woman he loved because of his own impulses.

It's taken you long enough to admit that you love her.

How could he admit to love when he barely knew the woman? He'd known the girl, the frightened, quiet, mouse-like girl who had hidden from the stares, bitten back comments instead of defending herself, and fled from the tormenting remarks of those around her.

Because he'd always known, somehow from the very day they had first met he had been in love with her.

She could've spent the rest of her life as a shy, quiet, and very vulnerable young woman. Instead she'd found the strength within, fought past the hatred and pain to become a woman any man in his right mind would be proud to have in his life.

She fights back now, when she's not being trapped by an alpha. And like it or not, Craig has the potential to become a full one. He can smell her -- the need, the heat, the readiness. Call it what you will, but your female is ready to be taken as a mate and he knows it.

She sat, half pinned on the railing, Craig in front of her, his hand tracing her face, cupping the cheek of the woman that belonged to him.

No.

He wasn't going to just sit back and let him maul his mate like that.

Control the anger. Don't let it out. A change now, with his anger so close to the surface, would be a disaster.

He took a long, slow breath, bringing the torrent of emotions under control before he actually spoke.

"Simone, we're leaving."

"So soon? What if she wants to stay? We're in the middle of something here." Craig turned, lowering his hand from her face.

"Are you sure about that? It looked like a conversation. Not exactly life threatening and something that could wait for another time."

"And if she wants to stay?" Craig smiled, turning to look at him fully. "I'm sure you could wait for a while, or I could take her home if you wanted to leave."

Kyle had controlled her life, given her no choices, and had laid down demands on her to go where he wanted when he wanted. Victor wanted her with him, but needed to show her he wasn't going to be like the man she'd left. Alpha needs warred with all-too-human desires.

"If Simone wants to stay a little longer I'd be willing to wait, but I promised to show her something after the party so it would be wrong of me to leave without her." He forced the anger and tension from his words, meeting Simone's wary gaze head on. "I don't want to force you to do anything you're not willing to do, Simone. I'm not like that."

He wanted to take her, move her away from Craig, cradle her against his chest as he inhaled the soft, sweet scent of her body. His. His mate. His female. His to protect and care for, but only if she would accept him.

"I want you to leave." A woman's tense voice carried into the conversation. "I made that very clear to you. However, I won't force Simone to leave the party just because you decided to act like a jerk."

Ann. Blast her. She stood there, arms folded beneath her breasts, defiant and angry even now. She glowered, her gaze moving from him to Simone and Craig, then back again. Separate and destroy. Find some lies to whisper into Simone's ears and push her toward Craig. He didn't have to hear the words to see the plans in her eyes.

"I see." He looked back at Simone. "Did you want to stay, or will you allow me to keep my promise to you?"

Chapter Fourteen

Leave, stay, listen to one story, or hear another. Craig, at least, had moved away from her, but now her body ached with the need to feel again. With Kyle she had never felt so alive, not the way she did now and with two men who could spark the fires in her being, who only had to look at her in order for her to crave being touched, kissed, and held. She didn't know what to do.

What was she turning into that two different men left her craving their touches, within moments of being with the other? A brief touch, a kiss, and she was left craving so very much more.

Breathe, take it slow and think ...

If she rushed into something now she'd regret it. Regret what? The feel of a hard cock sliding between her thighs, lips nibbling along her throat, strong hands caressing her body, lifting her into the heights of passion, pleasure, and the release she craved?

Images flashed through her mind. She could almost feel what it would be like. How she might be trapped between two men, both wanting her, needing her, soft growls against her flesh followed by strong touches that left her arching from one man to the next.

Her nipples crinkled, hardened points that pressed into the soft summer dress.

It no longer mattered that they were not alone. Save for the hatred she all but felt from that one who had sent her home in tears a hundred times and more during her younger years.

Yet now she knew what it was like to be the center of delicious attention.

How many years had she dreamed of this?

But now. Gods, now. If she could run, hide from this, she would do so in an instant. This felt so very good, yet wrong, all at the same time.

Then there was Ann. The other woman's gaze had hardened,

lines crinkling about her eyes. Hatred, anger, and frustration. Ann's lips moved without sound. Plans forming, cast aside without a word. She wasn't going to drop it. Not after the way she'd been cast aside so publicly by Victor. And now seeing Craig hit on Simone as well -- it had to irk Ann.

Staying wasn't an option.

"I'll go with you," she murmured. Better to leave and let him gain the chance of keeping his promise than to close the door in his face.

An indrawn hiss of breath.

Craig.

"Are you sure? I'll take you home after the party if you want to stay." He reached out, running his fingers over her arm. Gods, even with the delight of his touch, a part of her still felt cold. "There is so much we can learn about each other, history we need to share. I want to spend the time with you, to be given the chance to get to know you. And for you to come to know me. Give me a chance. That's all I ask."

She desired him, yet it was Victor her gaze was drawn to far more than Craig. Victor whose presence commanded her attention.

"I'm sure." She nodded. Victor, his touch only warmed; he'd not tried to make a move on her when she wasn't ready. Craig hadn't lied about them both needing her, but Victor at least seemed willing to let her set the pace to some degree.

Was this what love was? Being needed?

No, there'd been no mention of love.

From either of them. Just hints of something far more powerful than she understood.

"All right, but I'd like to meet you for coffee, tomorrow, if you're up to it." Craig shot a cold look at Victor, almost daring him to protest at the offer.

Keep the peace, agree, that's what she'd have done only a few months ago, before she'd had the nerve to leave Kyle. Not now.

Scars

"No, I don't think so."

"Why not?" He grasped her arm, fingers threatening to leave bruises in their wake. "Are you afraid of spending a little time with me? I won't harm you."

"Let go of me, Craig." She tugged at the grip, trying to slide free of his hold. Fear nibbled at the back of her mind. Memories of another man, one who never let her go no matter how much she pleaded with him, or cried.

"You heard the lady. Let her go." Victor took a step forward. "She said no, and she wants to leave with me." Low voice, barely more than a whisper, but the threat was there and the promise of danger, action that would be taken if Craig ignored his words. It should've frightened her, warned her off, a protective streak in him that would be so easy to turn into the controlling, abusive man she'd been with.

No. He wasn't Kyle.

Craig held the potential to be like Kyle, but Victor offered her protection. Did Craig fear her would-be knight?

"And if I want to talk with her?"

"That has to be her choice, but for now she appears to wish to leave with me." Victor's voice remained calm, despite the hidden threat of a struggle between the two men. A fight over her?

Men didn't fight or argue over the likes of her. Men preferred Ann's type of beauty. Her wealth and position, her pretty unmarked face, the car, dresses, the right connections.

Yet there they stood. All but fighting for a moment of her time.

"For now, then," Craig nodded, releasing his grip on her. "You and I will talk later. I'll wait until you're ready, but we will be having that conversation."

"Maybe." The time for backing down had gone. "But try and push me around like that again, Craig, and you'll regret it. I don't like men who act that way." Snakes writhed in her stomach, a cold sweat coating the back of her neck. If he struck or growled, she wasn't sure what she'd do.

Stop, apologize, and make it up to him.

No, she wasn't that fearful child anymore.

"Are you sure you know what you're doing here?" Craig's eyes locked with hers, waiting for her to back down. "I could be everything you wanted in a man and your worst nightmare if you make a mistake."

Hated images flashed through her mind. Fists. Closed hands. Knuckles that slammed into her face. Every blow, each cruel word and the spat accusations that laid the blame on her shoulders. Days spent hiding until the bruises had healed. Moments curled up in the bath, looking at the razor in her hand, hoping to find a way to end it, only to know she couldn't do a thing about it. The coward's way out, but it would still have been a way to escape. No more. She'd been down that road. Never again.

She moved without thinking, her hand grasping his cloth-covered balls, squeezing, twisting them. A voice not her own spilled from her lips, giving life to words she'd never dreamed of speaking. "Back off. You've no idea just what my worst nightmares contain. But I'll make this very plain. Using small words so you don't have any doubt about my words. Touch me again without my permission, and I'll rip these off, then present them to you on a chain. Is that clear?"

Chapter Fifteen

Gravel crunched under the tires as they fled the party. "I never thought I would see the day that someone took Craig down publicly." Victor made no attempt to keep the smile from his face.

Did she not know the courage she had shown? Or how he had wanted to howl in sheer delight at her actions?

With such a woman at his side, his place at the head of the pack could not be denied. No man or woman, alpha or beta, would challenge him.

"I didn't think I had it in me, or that I'd stand up to someone in such a way, not ever." She shifted in the passenger seat, heat flushing across her cheeks. He'd never have thought it of her, not in a million years. Not even with the strength he had seen, half hidden beneath the surface. Not after everything she had been through, the strength beaten down, hidden, locked away until he thought he would never see it freed.

"Well, you have, and you did. You caught me off guard with your actions, and as for Craig ... well it was an interesting sight to see." He couldn't stop smiling. Craig had blustered, stepped back, ready to agree to anything she had wanted from him. He'd given his word without hesitation, just as long as she released that tight and painful grip from his balls.

And she had. Only to look him straight in the eyes before turning and leaving on Victor's arm. Strong, confident, ready to stand up to other males in the pack. She was going to be one hell of an alpha female, just as long as he could persuade her to be his mate.

The scant doubts he'd held about her ability to be his mate had faded. Such a beauty. A woman that he would love and protect until the end of his days.

"So what did you plan on showing me, or explaining to me?" Her words broke through his thoughts.

"Shortly. We need to go somewhere first."

"Victor, if you keep jerking me around like this, I'll get out of the truck and walk home."

"I'm not jerking you around. Just, this involves showing you something, and I can't do it here. I promised you and I'm going to keep that promise." That newfound strength called to him, tugging on his soul. Powerful, more so than any perfume or even the heated scent of sheer desire.

His cock strained at his jeans, his gaze pulled toward the soft skin of her breasts, dark points of her nipples pressed against her dress. That graceful arc of her throat, slender thighs, a confidence now pulsing through her body with each strong beat of her heart. Each touch of air through the window pulled wild, unseen fingers through her hair.

Beautiful.

"You're asking me to trust you an awful lot for someone who just got his face slapped in the middle of the party." She muttered, leaning back in the seat. "Then again, I'm one to talk, after what I just did. Damn. I don't know what came over me, but whatever it is I like it. Gods, I enjoyed it. I loved seeing the fear in his eyes. He backed down; I've never made a man back down like that before. Kyle, I had learned. I knew which buttons to push with him, how to work it so I could leave. But I don't know Craig. How did I know it would work?"

She took a long, slow breath before she continued, her voice trembling.

"I'm shaking like a leaf, Victor. How could I enjoy doing that to him?"

"I can understand that, and you did nothing wrong, believe that. He's had it coming." So much had changed for her, and too fast for most to be able to cope. Yet she'd adapted, accepted it, and tried to work with it. Did she not know how rare that ability was?

Of course not. She didn't see her worth, know it, or

understand it. Not yet, at least. No one had ever taken the time to show her, to teach her just how much she had to offer the world.

"It'll be all around town by this time tomorrow. How will I face everyone then? With them knowing what I did to him?"

"Not if Craig has anything to do with it. He won't want others knowing about it, and he'll do everything he can to squash the rumors." He smiled, hoping to calm her nerves at least a little.

"But what about those who saw it?" She turned, looking fully at him. "Surely ..."

"Most will back down when Craig tells them to."

"Oh." Disappointment flared in her gaze. "Well, perhaps that's for the best."

"Maybe." He wasn't so sure. Craig needed to be brought down hard and fast. If he stopped the story from being spread, then it would be Victor's delight to make sure that the rest of the pack knew. It was just one more way to keep the other man in his place, as the beta, not a full alpha acknowledged by the pack, yet still strong enough to be his second.

Dangerous game to play, but it might be the way to keep him in line without weakening the pack as a whole. Good. You're learning.

"I don't understand why Ann wanted me to stay at the party."

"Head games. I arrived with you; pushing me out and you staying might have forced you into something with Craig. Or at least given her the opening to plant some rumors. Remember how she works. 'Look how fickle his date was. I kicked him out and she was straight on to the next man.'"

"Bloody bitch, she'd try that, and I almost ..."

"Fell for it?"

"Yes, I wasn't thinking very straight at first." She frowned, looking out of the window. "Where are we going?"

"My farm; it's nothing special, but it's the best place to show you what's going on." Trust, she had to trust him, if only for a little longer. Gods, she'd panic when she saw him in his true form. Run from him, or reach for a gun, or a club.

What other choice did he have?

"I see, and there's no other place to explain things?" A hint of nerves?

"Not really ..."

"Craig told me he needed me as well, that you both did, so whatever this is involves him as well?"

What else had he told her? "Yes, it does."

"And others?" She pressed a little further.

"What did he tell you?" Panic dried his mouth out.

Calm yourself, if she knew she'd have laughed in his face, not just tried to yank his balls off, though I admit that was a sight well worth seeing. Perhaps she'll do a repeat performance on you?

"Is there someone else here?" She frowned, twisting in the seat, looking back. "Or a radio you left on. I swear I can hear a buzzing sound, not all the time though."

Oh boy, this is going to be interesting.

How could she hear the other?

Was that even possible?

She's an alpha in the making, a female strong enough to bring new blood into the pack without being swallowed whole. Of course she's going to have some of our gifts before she changes.

"There it is again."

"It will all make sense soon, I promise." Sure, a voice in the back of his head that she could sense, maybe even hear, and if things went well he'd be biting her, helping her through her first change and claiming her as his mate. Oh sure, shape shifting into a wolf made a lot of sense, if you were drunk or had spent too many years reading horror novels.

It still didn't explain how she could hear or sense his advisor. He wasn't able to hear the others that spoke to the pack. They couldn't hear the one that he was forced to listen to.

Quit whining; you're a grown male, not some cub needing his sire. Don't you know that female alphas are different?

Scars

His jaw tightened, teeth grinding. He turned the truck off the highway and onto the narrow track that led up to the farm. How many generations of his family had lived and died here? Four, five? He'd never asked, but the farm was old enough to have seen that and more.

And it will see many more to come, cub.

He wasn't a damn cub.

Then stop acting like one.

"When did he die?"

"Who?" The question caught him off guard, the engine dying as they pulled up outside the brown and cream-colored building.

"Your father. I know your mom's been gone for twenty years or so."

"A couple of years now; he'd been ill for a long time."

"Cancer? I mean, I know he didn't die of that, but when you say he'd been ill ..."

"No. I'd rather not talk about it."

"Why not? He was a good man. You shouldn't just shut him out of your life now that he's dead."

"Because there are other things I want to talk to you about first." He slid out of the truck, closing the door behind him. "And talking about him won't bring him back."

"Stubborn bastard."

"Yes, I am. You'll get used to that with me."

Peaceful, he'd heard the word used about the farm a dozen times, known it to be a safe haven, one of the few places the pack didn't try and jostle each other for power. Right now he'd have happily faced off Craig in a fight rather than go through this with Simone.

Like you ever need an excuse to think about fighting Craig?

"All right, we're here. What is it you need to tell me?"

"Part tell, part show." It wasn't even close to being dark but at least here he could shift without the open risk of being caught. "My family is a little different. We've been living with a gift, a curse if you will, that has affected us for more generations than we have been able to track."

"What are you talking about?" She frowned, following him as he walked slowly past the house, toward the pasture at the far side. "You're not making a lot of sense here. In fact you're making me feel a little unsettled."

There was little point in putting it off any longer.

"I'm a werewolf."

"You're a what?" She blinked, looking at him before blinking again. "Okay, you can bring out the cameras now, and the caught-on-TV cast."

"This isn't a joke. Craig, me, Steve, and a few others are shifters, werewolves in our case, though there are others who can shape shift into different forms. None of them live locally, though, not since the pack had a run-in with a werelynx a few years ago."

She didn't move, or speak, not for several long minutes. Disbelief and shock registered in her eyes. A soft breeze played through her hair, tugging at it, pulling the long, loose strands across her face.

"You're insane." she whispered. "Totally insane. You actually believe this."

"I wish I was. I might be many things, but I'm not insane." How could he tell her the worst of it, that one of his kind, Craig, the very man who would want to take her from him, was the one who'd marked her face? "I can prove it."

"How? You have a costume somewhere in the house?" She folded her arms under her breasts, a stubborn look crinkling the tiny lines about her eyes. "Is this some sort of kinky sex game?"

"No, it's nothing like that. I meant I can prove it, and I can. Like this."

A risk, to force the change, one he knew would hurt -- but when didn't it hurt?

Give yourself to the wolf, let him flow through your body and bring the change. Feel the dirt beneath your paws, extend

Scars

your claws, feel the grit and taste the pleasures offered to you. Stronger, faster, better than anything else on this world. A wolf, leader, hunter, fighter and a protector. Bold, strong, and brave.

Pain rippled through his body, skin splitting, clothing shredding. Normally he would have stripped off, but she was doubtful enough as it was. He had enough time to kick of his shoes before his feet began to shift.

Forget about the petty things. Better to be the wolf than human, to feel the pulse of the earth through your veins. Fur, teeth, claws, and the rush of life.

Life, death, all the same thing.

She screamed, terror carried by the cry.

Dirt beneath his paws, a howl, pain lancing through his body, tail forcing from nowhere, until his head lifted to the sky and a cry, the full-throated worship of a wolf, rang out across the pasture.

A sound that broke through her stunned fear and sent her running back toward the truck. Not exactly what he had in mind.

Hopefully she doesn't find that gun you have under the seat.

Chapter Sixteen

Werewolf? Okay, she'd heard some stories in her time, but this was nuts. At best, a joke, a sick one. At worst, a way of trying to get her into bed, not that she could see it working. Not even with the way she craved his touch.

She fought back the urge to laugh at him, waiting for the punch line, the next move, only to feel her heart turn to lead.

His skin shifted, shredding as she watched. Blood, skin, cloth rippled away from his form, fur pushing through. Teeth, paws, and claws.

Shit. What was happening?

Had he drugged her?

His shoes, he'd kicked his shoes off, sending them toward her. His body shifting, changing before her eyes; his hands turning into paws, claws that dug into the dirt beneath him.

A tail? My gods, that was a tail, a real one.

Hazel eyes. Gold flecks.

His eyes. Victor's eyes stared back at her from the face of the beast.

She screamed, hands clenching at her sides. A dog -- no, a wolf. Gods, a wolf. Why couldn't he have been lying? A twisted joke? Or a way to get into her pants. That would have been easier than this. Than seeing him shift into being a wolf.

He'd kill her.

That's why he needed her, to feed.

Hunger.

Wolves ate people.

She screamed before she knew it, turning as she ran toward the truck. The keys. Gods, let him have left the keys in the truck. She had to get out of here, away from him, it, whatever he was now.

Why had she listened to him? Staying at the party would have been better than facing this nightmare.

He growled, appearing in front of her, blocking her path to the truck, his teeth bared. He'd strike and rend into her body with the very claws she had seen take shape. She knew how that felt. Not again, she couldn't do it again. Simone stumbled backwards, fighting to keep from cowering in a ball. She'd meet him on her feet, not just wait to be killed, or bitten.

A piece of wood, something.

There had to be a bar, or wood, crowbar, or better yet a shotgun she could use against him.

He didn't move. As long as she didn't try and dart for the truck he made no fresh move toward her. Why?

If he wanted to strike, he could do so now. She couldn't stop him. No weapons, no way of defending herself from a bite, or his claws. So why didn't he move?

"Well, are you going to get on with it, or just stand there and stare at me?"

He grinned, the damn thing had just grinned at her.

"What's so funny?" A shovel, pitchfork, there'd be one somewhere on the farm. If she could get hold of one, then she could chase it away.

He sat down, tail wagging with those large hazel eyes fixed on her.

"Dammit, can't you talk like that?"

A soft, mournful howl was the only answer. Of course he couldn't talk in this form. Wolves didn't talk anyway. They growled, snapped, and bit into people, but they didn't hold conversations with people.

A wolf. Like the one that had attacked her as a child.

Not a dog, but a wolf.

Memories flooded back into her mind.

The large creature that had burst into her bedroom, coming through the window, eyes wild. The growl, a warning she'd not heeded. Not in time to prevent it from striking her. Pain, those claws burning a path across her face, tearing into her skin, blood, blood everywhere, on her lips, in her eyes and staining her nightgown.

Wolves, howling outside. A fight, between two or more of them.

No. Not that. Not a dog, not a true wolf, but one of these creatures? She'd been attacked by a werewolf in her own home.

"Oh, gods, you were there that night."

He nodded slowly, lowering his head to the ground, whining.

"Keep away from me." She took a step back, cold beads of sweat; her hands seeking something to strike at him with. Had he been the one that had attacked her? "Please, keep away from me."

Another whine pierced the air. With a mournful look in his large, soft eyes, he crept toward her on his belly. With his liquid eyes and his tongue sliding out between his teeth, there was nothing threatening about him.

So why was she shaking so badly?

Memories. Nothing but bad memories. He wasn't going to hurt her.

"You want me to trust you, after you've just turned into a beast?" Sharp teeth, dangerous claws, he could kill her in a moment.

So why didn't he?

Victor whimpered, then shook his head. His form rippled, fur shedding, his tail slowly receding into his body. A low cry of pain, a howl as the wolf became a man. Strong, tanned, lines of muscles clear across his chest. Her gaze lingered on his body, tracing a slow pattern down his chest and lower. A blush claiming her cheeks as she realized not only was he beautiful but Victor was also very naked.

Well formed. She'd heard the term before. Now she could see the meaning behind it. Long legs, toned, taut muscles that glistened from beads of sweat left over from the change. A patch of tight curled hair between his thighs, and a strong erection that refused to let her look away.

"No, I'm asking you to trust me because I'm telling you the truth."

Her lips moved, throat refusing to work. Her hands itched with the need to feel his cock between them, stroking it, exploring it. What would it feel like in her mouth or driving into her clenching sex?

Warmth built through her body, heated, wet, a throbbing she couldn't deny. Nipples crinkled under the thin summer dress, skin tingling with the images of his body pressed against hers, his cock sliding between her thighs, claiming her, rubbing into her sex. Taking every part of her until she screamed in desire.

No, don't think about it. He's a freak, a monster ...

Gods, wasn't that exactly what they'd called her?

Chapter Seventeen

Fear and lust? He could smell both coming from her. Drawing him like nectar would a bee. She didn't step back from him despite the strength of fear that gripped her. Neither did she give into the lust. Her nipples hardened under the yellow dress, her thighs clenched tight as her breath came in soft, rapid gulps.

Did she know just how soft and vulnerable she now looked to him as she fought against the double need that assaulted her being? How could she control it? The desire should have overwhelmed her to the point of near insanity.

"I'm not going to hurt you." He half reached out for her, then pulled back. No brushing her face, no matter how tempting it was. It might be too much right now. Her skin was so soft, tempting. Almost like silk beneath his fingers.

"Yes, you will, like the one that jumped into my room! You and your kind attacked me. I know that's what happened. I can remember it now. The howling, the wolves that hid outside my window, for all I know it was you that left me looking like this." She brushed her fingers over the scars.

She had no idea how those scars failed to repulse him. The spirit guide was right. What were a few scars amongst his kind? Most adult wolves carried a few, from hunting, fighting, accidents during their early years. They just didn't matter to him.

"Not me. I didn't enter the house and the rest of the pack punished the one involved as soon as we could." Would she believe him? The risk was ever present that she would refuse him, blame him for what had happened during her childhood. "I know who did it, and he's still alive. The pack wouldn't kill him because he was just a cub at the time. He was still learning what it meant to be one of us, how to control the power in his body."

"Cub? That thing couldn't have been a baby. It was huge." She protested. "If it had been that young, it should have been tiny, not that monster of a thing."

"To a small child, yes, he would have been. The cub ... he wasn't quite ten at the time, but it wasn't an excuse, and even then we knew you were important to the pack." He took a step closer, reaching out for her. She didn't move, though the fear oozed from her along with the raw sexual need. She might as well have been naked for all the protection her clothing offered. "We mature quickly in some ways, less so in others."

"I'm not sure what you mean."

"We come into physical maturity quickly; that's the nature of animals. But we're still human, so we have to deal with the problems of the human lack of maturity. The urges to do foolish things. Take risks that an adult wouldn't."

"And why am I important?"

"New blood for the pack." New blood, new power, an alpha and a woman that the male members of the pack might be driven to kill over. Either to claim or protect. The very thought of someone else finding her, bringing her over and perhaps taking her from the boundaries of their lands, their hunting grounds, was almost too much to bear.

"You're going to kill me?" A low moan, a backward step that almost sent her stumbling to the ground, or would have if he hadn't grabbed her arm. "Please, don't kill me, Victor. I won't tell anyone about you, about this. Oh, gods."

Did she really think he would do that?

The terror in her eyes screamed yes.

"No, not kill you. I need you, want you. A lover, mate, my partner -- all the things you should have been able to find in the city but couldn't. I want a life with you. I need that." His arms wrapped about her, drawing her against his chest, one hand sliding into her hair. Soft, silken, her body shook in his arms, her breath a warm, sultry caress against his skin that urged him onward.

No, she wasn't ready. He had to wait until she gave herself to him.

"Why me?"

"Wolf blood. Your grandmother was a shifter, like us. She took a nonshifter as a mate. It was dormant in your mother, but she'd have still worked. In you, though, it's alive, viable, calling to every one of us." Every shifter in the area, and then some. Why that blood hadn't attracted shifters in the city, he couldn't be sure.

Dammit all, they were running out of time.

With our sense of smell would you honestly risk living in a place as smelly as the cities?

It had a point.

It? I'm a he, not an it. Really, cub, I would have thought you might have learned a few basic manners by now.

"I'm just the chance to spawn more of your kind?" Doubt flared into life.

"No, it's more than that. You only have to walk into a room, and I want to hold you, pull you close to me, kiss you, and so much more." So easy, it would've been so easy to just kiss her. "You've no idea just how hard it is for me to resist that. Craig would have felt the same thing. The pull. It's like a drug. No, that's the wrong word, but I don't have a word for what being around you does to me."

So do it, then. Kiss her. And you know what she does to you; take a look down. That's no stick you're wandering around with, poking her. But you could still, well ... I'm sure you get the picture.

No, it wasn't the time.

She clung to him, shaking, hardened nipples scraping against his chest, her nails digging into his skin, his cock pressing between her thighs. Seeking the entrance to bliss that her body offered him without speaking.

A low groan, almost a growl, need and desire blended as she fueled his passions. He had to keep it under control.

A heady scent wrapped about her body, calling to him. It coated her skin, hair, and overwhelmed her very existence.

Scars

Desire swept away control and need destroyed reason.

His hand moved into her hair, tightening, tipping her head backwards, and then he crushed his lips down on hers. They parted beneath his touch, welcoming his tongue as it slid against hers, stroking, exploring the tender insides of her mouth. A low shudder, a whimper; she tensed for a moment in his arms, almost ready to fight before she melted against him, suckling on his tongue with a hunger of her own.

"No." His voice, not hers.

"What? What did I do wrong?"

"Nothing, I'm pushing you into this." He broke his hold on her, stepping back, barely aware that he still stood buck naked out in the middle of the pasture. "You're not ready."

"I am. I ..."

"It's the power of the wolf blood in you." He shook his head, fighting for control. Sweet, heady, the scent pulsed into the air with every breath she took. "It's not just me it affects, but you as well. You're ready to mate, you want to, but you're afraid. Afraid I'll treat you like he did."

"So show me you're not like him. Please."

Chapter Eighteen

She reached out to him, her fingers entwining with his as she pulled him close. Callused hands, worker's hands, a body that felt warm as he wrapped his arms about her. Love, desire, did it matter what it was he felt toward her?

"Show me! Please, love me and show me what it can be like with a man that isn't out to hurt me or control me." She needed this, needed to know that such a thing was possible. That all her fears, the terror Kyle had left her with when it came to men, could finally come to an end.

No words, just a low growl of triumph. He urged her back toward the damp grass, her thighs parting under his touch, hips rocking up against him. Fingers moving to the slender straps of her summer dress, slipping it down from her breasts, then bunching her skirt about her hips.

"I've wanted you for so very long now." Soft lips caught her throat, kissing, nibbling along the line of her jaw. "All those years of watching you grow up, knowing that I couldn't tell you, knowing you feared the creatures that had attacked you."

Wolf, large hazel eyes, human eyes, but he'd been a wolf. Fear surged into being, only to die under the soft assault of his lips.

"You've no idea what I've been dreaming through the years. I didn't dare say anything." She murmured, leaning into his touch, craving more of his soft tender kisses. The gentle feel of his lips, his teeth over her throat, down toward her breasts. "Every girl wanted you, but I knew you'd never look my way."

"Wrong. You couldn't have been more wrong, Simone." His lips caught about one nipple, suckling it into his mouth with a low growl. Her name, gods, he'd said her name as if it were almost a prayer. He clawed at her sides, holding her to him. Warmth, tingling, a deep pulling sensation rippled through her body, shooting down into her core, soaking her inner walls. Teeth grazed over the ripe nub, nipping, hard enough to turn a moan into a soft yelp.

"Please." So damn good. She'd never felt so needed, or alive, as she did in this moment.

"Soon," he growled against her breast. "When you're ready, truly ready." A line of kisses and light bites trailed from one breast to the other before his teeth caught the unclaimed nipple.

She cried out, arching beneath him, her nails scraping down his back. She could feel him, his cock pressing between her thighs; he wanted her, needed her, so why didn't he take her now?

Lightning bolts of heat flashed down across her stomach, tightening, rippling through her body. She couldn't hold back, but he wanted her to. Long, slow kisses marked a lingering path over her stomach, wet trails that left her shivering, pressure building between her thighs. And still he continued.

His hands parted her thighs, warm, damp breath whispering over her mound, down between her lower lips. A caress that tore a low cry from her mouth, hips arching, pressing upward. Heat, liquid velvet heat threatened to coat her inner thighs, muscles tense as she pressed tight against him, waiting for that intimate touch.

It never came.

His lips pressed against her inner thigh, suckling, nipping, and nibbling a long trail down her leg. A path of desire laid out over her skin, each bite, each nip, leaving her arching, needing more, wanting a way to sate the pressure in her body. Soft kisses traced the side of her knee, down over her calf, covering her with his touch, tasting every part of her, yet never touching the aching need within her clenching vulva.

He reached up, hooking his fingers into the sides of her panties, scooting them downward, easing them from her body as she whimpered under his insistent caress.

Soft kisses covered the sole of her foot, sensations turning from pleasure into near pain before merging back into the warmth of purest delight as she struggled not to yank her foot back from his grip. Normally ticklish, she raised her hips toward the sky as his suckling kisses against the tender arch of her foot left her groaning.

"What are you doing to me?" Her body felt alive, every inch of her skin tingled in anticipation of the next touch, and she didn't care about the beast that lurked beneath his skin, just as long as he continued. Pressure rose, like a hidden hand between her thighs, cupping her pussy lips, brushing over them, squeezing her inner walls with the drive to feel him buried within her writhing body.

"Loving you," he murmured, smiling as he shifted to her other foot, beginning his long, slow journey upward. "Showing what it means to be in the arms of one who needs you, who would never hurt you."

She couldn't take the wait any longer. With a low groan she sat up, her fingers tangling into his hair, pulling him toward her, thighs parting wide. "I need you, now."

"Impatient." He settled between her thighs, rubbing the head of his cock against her slick, heated lips. "Maybe I should make you wait a little longer, until you're ready to scream my name."

Scream? She'd hire a publicist and paint his name in mile-high red letters in the middle of the town if only he'd slide that delicious cock where it belonged.

"Evil," she groaned, tracing her nails over his back, locking her heels behind his taut, rounded ass, trying to force him in. "Wicked, evil, teasing man."

"Sounds like words of love to me." He leaned down, nipping her throat. "Not quite ready, are you? You can tell me. I haven't managed to arouse you yet."

Was strangling your lover for not fucking you classed as self-defense, or just a moment of sheer insanity?

"If this isn't being aroused, then I don't know what is."

"You'll find out, my word on it." He leaned up, taking his

weight on his hands as he looked down at her. "You're beautiful, Simone. Bold, bright, stronger than any woman I've ever met."

"No, I'm not."

"You are, and if it takes me until the end of my days to help you see that, then that's what I'll do." He thrust forward, pressing into her sex in a long, deep rock. Filling her beyond anything she had known before.

"Gods!" She arched up, hands clenching into his body, hips rocking against him. Complete. Her walls tightened against his cock, claiming him, closing on his throbbing erection, ankles locked behind his ass. "Need you, I need this with you."

His teeth closed on her throat, hips rocking deeper into her body, stretching her sex, filling her with each deep thrust. "So tight, warm." His teeth released their grip only to find a new place to bite, sinking into the tender spot between her neck and shoulder. "Mine."

His. Yes, his!

She reached out, moving her hands back up his back, into his hair, down over his ears, massaging his lobes, pressing in firm circles, only to feel him shudder, a low, snarling growl gaining life from the back of his throat. She'd never known a man to react so deeply to having his ears touched.

Steady thrusts changed, turning into a deep grinding, hips circling, driving into her sex. He'd been holding back, and so had Simone.

With her ankles locked behind his ass, her fingertips massaging his shoulders, she pressed upward, twisting her hips, dancing on his cock, her slick walls tightening, rippling, releasing only to clench again on him.

A growl, almost a howl, pressure building between them, her body tight, needful and alive. Blood raced through her veins, throbbing with each rapid beat of her heart. Fear rose and died in a moment. She'd never known such an onslaught of pleasure and pressure combined. A power that controlled her had been unleashed from the deepest cage in her being. Now it dominated her body, forcing her to move, clench on him, and seek a place to bite.

Her teeth sank into his chest as he cried out. His matching bite on her shoulder, thighs tight, a joint scream echoing through the pasture. Liquid heat washed over her inner walls, coating his cock as he pulsed, shuddering into her, neither one caring about the pain of the bites. Only for the moment. Pure bliss, sexual release, his, hers, it didn't matter right now, not even when they both collapsed on the thick, damp grass.

Chapter Nineteen

"Wow." He sighed into her hair, inhaling the sweet mixture of sex and sweat.

Is that all you have to say. You've been waiting for how many years to get her and all you have to say is wow?

"Thank you." She turned, nestling into his arms.

"For what? I should be thanking you." Victor smiled, pulling her close until her head rested on his chest.

"For reminding me that not all men are like Kyle." Her breath caressed a path across his chest. "I needed that."

"Hush, there's no need to speak about him, is there? He's gone. Nothing more than a memory of the past soon to be forgotten, if I have anything to say about it." His fingers slid through her hair, pulling out the tangles. "I want to just hold you here, until the end of days, but we can't."

"Why not?" A soft frown creased her brow.

"You mean apart from the damp grass, the cold, and the fact we're going to be attracting mosquitoes any moment now?"

"Yes." She rolled over, straddling his hips, her sex tantalizingly close to his still-hard cock. "Apart from all those minor details."

"Well, as much as I don't like to think about it, there's still the matter of the pack."

Her hand moved to the bite on her shoulder, color draining from her face. "You bit me." A soft shudder ran through her body. "I'm going to become one of you, aren't I?"

"You already were; you've just been waiting for the right moment to turn, to be shown the way home." Fear, he could smell it mingling with the remains of their shared passion, though far less than it had been earlier. "There's nothing to be afraid of. I won't let anyone harm you."

"And what about the one that managed to attack me as a child?"

He sighed then sat up, crossing his legs as he pulled her onto his lap. "He was looking for a mate, even then. Your mother was taken, and he was angry, frustrated, and like many a young beast he struck out without thinking. He never wanted to hurt you and certainly didn't want you dead."

"What happened to him?" She rested against his chest, closing her eyes as she listened.

"He was punished by the pack, forbidden the ability to shift until he turned eighteen."

"That's it? That's all that happened to him? He marked me for life."

"You're still very human; after you've taken wolf form a time or two, you'll understand. They're scars. They don't make you who you are; they only show some of what you've been through. Wolves are hunters, fighters. We don't go through life without gaining a few scars of our own, and we don't look on them the same way humans do. You're beautiful. I meant that when I said it. I still mean that."

If he had to tell her that every day for the rest of their life together, then so be it.

"I don't know ... I mean ... I've spent so long being judged by the marks on my face instead of for who I am inside." She blinked, tears shining on thick lashes, glimmering in the dying light of the sun. "I don't know if I have the strength."

He struggled against the urge to enfold her in his arms forever. Protecting her was only a small part of being a mate; he had to know when it was time to let her stand up to her fears.

"Simone, you're one of the strongest women I've ever known. You faced down Craig, and you left Kyle. You've come home and stood up to Ann in the middle of the street. Those things take guts, real determination." He cupped her chin, lifting her face up so he could look into her eyes.

"No, you're wrong. A strong woman wouldn't have let Kyle ..."

"Even strong men and women make mistakes. You overcame

it; you walked out, with your head held high. Don't knock yourself for that." His thumb brushed over the line of her jaw. "Look at me, look into my eyes, see what's there. I'm not lying to you, or hiding anything now. I see a woman who deserves a strong man who can walk at her side, who will take control of her own life, and who sometimes needs the arms of another to hold her. I only hope you'll let me be that man."

Her eyes closed, a soft shudder rocking through her half-naked body. Her dress had bunched as a yellow band of cloth about her waist, panties and shoes forgotten on the grass. Still they were in a better state than his clothes. "I think you're right; we should move inside, and I need to know what's expected of me now. How will the change happen, and what about the other members of the pack? Will they accept me, or try and force me to take a different mate?"

Real fears, the chances were slim but they still existed. If he had not been the alpha then he would've been forced to fight every member of the pack in order to keep her as his mate.

You might have to fight at least one member of the pack, though there is one other option. I can't see Craig just backing down to you, not when he's sensed the interest she has in him.

How could she be interested in the one who had attacked her? Besides she'd stood up to him, forced him to publicly back down. Didn't that mean she had rejected him?

He wants her; she's interested in him. He stands on the cusp between alpha and beta, able to step up to the mark with the right female, or back down.

Great, it was going to come down to a fight. An all-out struggle for the pack and his status.

Perhaps, perhaps not. A lot depends on the pretty little she-wolf you're about to introduce to the rest of the family.

No. The spirit was wrong there. Nothing would come between him and Simone. He wouldn't let it. Even if it did mean he had to show Craig his place in the pack once and for all. Or he could kick the troublemaker out to become a lone rogue.

"The only way they'll be able to do that is if you don't want me, or they find a way to kill me. You're mine, Simone, for as long as you'll have me."

Chapter Twenty

She didn't have the words to explain how she felt, the peace that he had given her, not after that. Nor even when he pushed up to his feet, lifted her into his arms, and carried her toward the house. He strode away from the pasture, leaving her panties and shoes, along with the shredded remains of his clothes, in the grass. Common sense said tell him to stop, to collect the clothing, her shoes, but she nestled against his chest instead, content to be in his arms.

What if someone came to the farm and saw her clothing, or his? Or both?

It wasn't like they were in the city; they'd hear a car approaching, and this was private property. People didn't just wander around someone else's farm without permission. Did they?

Her shoulder hurt, throbbing from the bite, a feverish chill touching her flesh. Should it burn like that?

"We'll get the bite cleaned up in a bit, once I get you in a bath."

"Bath?"

"Well, unless you find the idea of me bathing you to be repulsive?"

"Gods, no, never." Pass up the chance to feel his fingers moving over her body, soap, warm water, his hands cupping her breasts, easing between her thighs only to bring her sobbing into the aching delights he'd introduced her to in the pasture. Did he think she was insane?

Maybe he did and with good reason.

"Good, because I think you'll enjoy what I have in mind. Vanilla, real vanilla."

Real vanilla? Did people actually use that? He appeared to. That stuff was pricy, to say the least.

His bare feet slapped against the wood of the deck; a screen door creaked open to clap shut behind them as he carried her into the house. All these years and she'd never been inside his home before. Old lavender, chamomile and tea; so many different scents mixed, intense in a way they had never been before.

"Warm water, soap, and organic vanilla oil. It will help soothe you. Your body will be going through a few odd changes."

"Like my sense of smell increasing?" She looked up at him. He wasn't even straining from carrying her. Was that strength one he had been born with or something he had built up through hard work?

"That's part of it, some of it will hurt. I wish it didn't."

"Like changing form? That hurts, doesn't it? I heard it when you howled."

"Yes, it hurts, like fire moving through your body, exploding from fingers, toes. Every inch of your body screams in pain, if only for a few moments." He nudged a door open, carrying her into the bathroom and setting her down on a pile of clean towels.

Pain. She wasn't good with pain. Kyle had taught her that.

Yet for him, for Victor, she was willing to go through it. The pain meant she was a part of his world, that she'd been accepted.

"You learn to channel it, into the howl, a scream. It lets you know you're alive." He glanced back, offering a smile as he reached into the tub, turning the faucets on. Steam curled upward in soft tendrils that filled the air. Victor picked up a glass bottle of vanilla pods in oil and sprinkled drops of scented, yellow-tinged oil into the frothy water.

"Why a bath and not a shower?" She seldom allowed herself the luxury of just lying around in a tub. Relaxing too much left her open to be attacked by Kyle, so she'd given it up, opting for quick showers taken in stolen moments.

"It will ease the tension that's building up."

"Oh, can't we find another way of ..."

"It's not that kind of tension. Close your eyes and explore your body with your mind. Become aware of every ache, pain, twitch of muscles, the smells and sensations; don't shut a single thing out if it comes from inside of you."

"What?" What was he talking about? Something other than the pain he had warned her about, that much was obvious.

"I know it sounds strange, but do it. I've not let you down yet, have I?"

She nodded, closing her eyes, trying to ignore the wave of discomfort. This was silly. So she'd been bitten during sex and she could smell things a little bit better now. It didn't mean she was going to turn into a ...

Vanilla, sweet and heady like candy, wrapped about her, a warm, welcoming embrace. Her stomach growled. Lips parted, she could taste the vanilla in the air. Steam caressed her body, silken touches, hair damp as the air grew heavy with moisture. Small, unseen beads formed on her skin, hair rising, trapping the water, holding it in place. The towels were thick, fluffy, soft cotton of the best quality. No colors, no smell of bleach or harsh laundry detergent. She couldn't be sure what had been used, but it felt good.

A cramp came from nowhere, rocking through her body from her stomach upward. Lances of pain arced through her body, tearing a cry free. Her fingers tightened, clawing at the air.

"Let it flow through you. Control it; don't let it control you." A low voice, comforting, barely speaking above a whisper, yet she heard it. She heard everything. The wind outside the house rustled through the trees; a loose shingle tapped in the same breeze, demanding attention; and water filled the tub and splashed along the slick sides of the bath. There, something new, a tap, no, a series of them, a mouse somewhere below the floor. Every sound, every scent, it was all hers to listen to, accept or ignore at her whim.

Knives dug into her body, cutting deeply across her stomach. Her hands wrapped tight about her gut as she buckled over on the towels.

Gods. It hurt. More than she had ever thought possible, yet she couldn't scream.

"Breathe, let it go. Don't let it rule you."

"Hurts."

"I know; I've been there with it." He scooped her up from the floor, lifting her into the water. "Just relax when you can. Unclench your muscles. Let the warmth hold you."

Silken, soft, oil and water coated her skin, hair, face. She sank into it and let herself go. His hands, the bath, trust. She had to trust him. He could help. Guide. Protect her.

"Burns," she hissed, water filled the bite, but she lacked the strength to move back out of the tub, or even lift herself up enough to free the mark from the water's touch.

"It will pass; in time it will pass." His fingers moved through her hair, soothing, gentling her the same way he might do a horse. Tension slipped from her body, a moment of peace that she welcomed despite the fever that surged into life, only to recede once more. "The fever is normal; the pain is also. Once the first set of changes have been completed, the pain will die until you shift shape."

"I don't like it," she mumbled, barely feeling his touch now, her body threatening to sink into a numb blanket.

"No one ever does."

Chapter Twenty-One

Strong, proud, she's everything the lead female needs to be. She's ideal.

Even in her sleep he could see that, and didn't need the soft voice at the back of his mind to remind him of the obvious. The pain had wracked its terrible course through her body, pushing until she'd cried out and slumped down into a deep and much needed sleep. She hadn't even whimpered when he'd lifted her from the bath, wrapped her in a thick clean towel, and carried her into his bedroom.

He'd seen it before, in others, how much energy the first stages of the change took out of a newly bitten. But it had passed -- or the worst of it had. Now she slept, wrapped in a dozen quilts to stave off the chills, propped up on three pillows, her hair a haphazard, almost tangled mess about her face, long lashes dark on her cheeks.

Like most women, no doubt she would want to brush her hair out, smooth out the tangles until she looked presentable. But to him she looked perfect. No, more than that.

Innocent.

I wouldn't call her that after what you two did out in the pasture. No, definitely not innocent. She's wild and passionate, a mate to match your spirit. She'll make you the envy of the pack, not that you aren't already.

Will she have her own voice?

I think so. You all do, after the first shift to your true form. Wait until you run through the forest with her at your side. Can you feel it, the way the loam will be under your paws? Her tail, eyes, the scent of her in heat, nothing like it, and when you take her as your mate for the first time.

No, any mating would be done in human form. He'd not give up the feel of her naked skin under his, or the taste of her nipple in his mouth. She'd moaned, arched to him, clung with a desire so strong that few could match it. Passion surged through his body, thickening his cock. Tempting, just to strip the bedding away from her, waken her under his touch so he could see the flame rising in her eyes as they opened to shake off the dreams he hoped to bring to life.

Kyle. The shadow of the man stopped him. He'd never met him, hoped he never would, but Simone had spoken of her mistreatment at his hands. What if he'd done something to her whilst she slept, leaving her to awaken in fear, pain and misery. She'd not know it was him instead of the bastard she'd left, and her reactions ...

Not something he would risk, not until he knew more about her.

Protective. Good, you'll need to be.

Craig. She'd find out the one that had hurt her all those years ago not only lived, but wanted her.

"Victor?" Barely more than a murmur. "Where are you?"

"I'm here. It's all right." He moved closer, brushing his hand over her brow. The fever had broken, color returning to her face. "You're looking better, love, a lot better."

"I feel it, just a little disoriented. Dizzy." She blinked, slowly. "This is normal?"

"That's part of it." He settled on the edge of the bed, lifting a glass of water to her lips. "Drink, just a little. Your body will need fluids."

She didn't fight him, taking the water in small sips before she rested back on the full pillows, her gaze lingering over his body. "You're still naked." She smiled, a teasing light touching her eyes. "Are you hoping for round two?"

"Maybe, when you're strong enough." The thought of pressing her back against the bed, nibbling down her throat, taking hold of her before claiming her for a second time sent a surge of desire through his cock, thickening it, until need threatened to push all other thoughts from his mind.

Tires, cars, the sound of a radio. Someone was coming down the drive. A vehicle that sounded familiar.

Ah. Yes, of course. He should have expected the arrival of that one.

"Here, throw these on. They should fit." He pushed up from the bed, rummaging through a drawer before throwing a pair of sweats and a T-shirt at her. Smaller than he'd worn in a long time, but one thing with a pack is that you learned to keep clothes for all shapes and sizes on hand. The younger ones especially didn't always remember to strip off before shifting.

Not that he had any room to talk after the pasture.

"Who is it?" She glanced toward the window.

"Craig. I know the sound of his car." He pulled on a pair of sweats, leaving off a shirt. "I had hoped he'd give us a little time before coming out here, but it doesn't look like we're going to be that lucky."

"After today I thought, well ..."

"That he'd give you a wide berth? He would, if you weren't the only potential alpha female around. He won't be alone either; one of his supporters, Steve or Paul, will be with him. Both are pretty young, two years or so younger than you. Not sure if you knew them from school or not." He glanced back in time to see her give a quick shake of her head. "They're young enough to follow someone not just because he has the potential to be alpha but because he seems cool, or the best man out there, or he's offered them some measure of freedom from the laws of the pack."

She slid from the bed, easing the sweats on, ducking her head under the shirt. "I don't understand. Aren't we mated yet?"

"Not until we pair up after your first shift, which I was hoping would be tonight."

"Would be? Has something changed?"

"If they don't find a way to stop us. Look, there's something you need to know about Craig."

"You mean apart from the fact that he's an asshole?"

"He's the one that attacked you that night."

"And he still thinks he has a chance with me?" One delicate eyebrow arched, her fingers running over the raised ridges on her face. "He did this to me, then has the nerve to come on to me as if I'd accept him?"

"Remember what I said -- scars don't have the same meaning with us as they do with some humans. He might not realize you'd be angry at him about it."

"Bullshit. He used to hear what they called me. He'll know damn well what I went through because of him." Her words slid into a growl, hands clenched at her sides. "Just because he's cute and I felt a moment of ..."

His jaw clenched.

"Sorry, I didn't mean that I'd be interested in him. Just that, well, I don't really know. I should want to rip his throat out. A part of me does, but the rest ..."

"I know. I'm just ... Never mind, we'll cross that together." He moved back to her, pulling her into his arms, fingers wrapped in her hair. "I won't let them separate us, Simone. Trust me on that."

Not even if it cost him his sanity. He'd waited far too long to find her, to feel the peace that her presence now hinted at, to just give it up without a fight.

"You won't let them?" She pulled back from his touch just enough to look up into his eyes. "I won't let them. I'm done being pushed around, and if they try anything with me, they're going to find out just how much of a bitch I can be."

Chapter Twenty-Two

The clothes felt odd and being without shoes should have felt worse, but instead that part seemed normal. She turned, looking toward the source of the new sounds. Craig and two others. She could smell them before Victor opened the door. Each man had his own scent. They were a little different, almost like a silent voice or fingerprint. Her world had opened up in a wave of sensation, and she struggled to separate it all out into information she could use.

"You bastard. You fucked her before anyone else could have the chance, didn't you? I can smell her on you." Craig snapped before the door had even been fully opened. What did it matter who she had ...

Of course, the pack. Sex formed a bond. These weren't just the normal sort of men who would pass a woman around. She was special. She held a power that called to them. No more the scar-faced hag, the taunted woman; they desired her. More than that, they needed her.

Three men. Craig she recognized straight off. Steve was a lingering memory from school, one of the ones that hadn't called her names. But Paul was an unknown. Silent yet all too deadly, by the way he walked. Graceful, the same way a ballet dancer moved, but with a knife's edge shining in his dark eyes.

Women would flock to him, just as soon as he learned how to use that cold charm to his advantage.

"And you don't enjoy every moment you can get in Ann's bed?" She spoke before Victor could.

"How in the ... he bit you?" Craig's eyes widened.

"Yes, and you can keep your protests to yourself now. I'm not impressed by them. Did you fuck her before the party, or just after to soothe your insulted manhood?" She smiled, watching them file into the kitchen as she settled herself on the edge of the table.

Dangerous game, but they wouldn't kill her.

Yet the confidence she now felt left her skin tingling. Like this, she could have taken on the world without a second thought.

"Silence your bitch, Victor." Craig glowered at her, jaw tight. "I didn't come here to deal with her back chat."

"Funny, anyone would think you're afraid of me, Craig."

"I'm not afraid of some little female." She could almost see it, his hackles rising. "You'll back down soon enough."

"You should be afraid of me, Craig. Because if you touch me without my permission or try and tell me what to do, I'll make that little ball-grabbing incident at the party look like a walk through the park compared to what I'll do to you." His scent turned bittersweet, sweat forming across his brow as he shifted his weight from one foot to the other. "You're afraid of me, Craig. You can bluster all you want, but you won't take me on."

"Males don't fight females; we fight each other for the right to take the mate we want." Craig couldn't look her directly in the eye. "I don't have to take you on; it's not the way of the pack."

"The only way you're going to be able to lay one finger on me is if I let you, and that's not going to happen. Not unless I'm dead." Even as she gave the words life, she knew them to be a lie. No matter how angry she was at the other man, or how hard her life had been because of the marks she had been left with, there was something about him that called to her.

Craig shuddered. "I'm a wolf, not a deviant. I don't go into that sex-with-the-dead thing."

"Keep that in mind the next time you look at me as if I'm a piece of free ass." Power. She'd never felt anything like this before. He'd come in ready to stand up to Victor, fight for his right to take her as a mate, only to find out she wasn't going to let him. "Or maybe I'll just rip out your throat ... no, I'll mark up your face the same way you did to me."

"You told her. You bloody bastard, you told her. No wonder she doesn't want anything to do with me. She's still human." Craig growled. Without another word, he launched himself at Victor, the change happening before her eyes. "How could I stand a chance at claiming her when you had to go and tell her about my mistakes?"

"She had the right to know."

"I'll rip you're fucking throat out for this."

"Come on, then, try it. See how far you get."

Two sets of human bodies shifted. It happened quickly this time, one moment she had been staring at two men, the next they had become wolves, their clothing shredded into piles on the floor even as one lupine body slammed into the other.

"Get back!" Steve waved at them.

"Open the door and get them out. They have to fight outside." Paul, it had to be Paul, but she couldn't be sure.

She darted toward the door, pushing it open as she heard the first of the growls, loud snarls and the taste of blood and fur in the air. She had to get them outside. At least there, the fight would cause less in the way of damage.

"Shift. Shift and move outside; they'll follow you. You're in heat. Don't you understand that? If you shift and go outside, then they'll have no other choice but to obey that call." Steve grabbed her, pulling her to one side on the deck, his fingers digging into her arms. "I can't get in the middle of it. Paul can't. You're the only one who can. So shift if you want to stop them from killing each other."

"I don't know how to shift!"

"What?" Shock registered in Paul's eyes. "Shit. You have to. I mean, it's the only chance we have."

"But I can't."

Yes, you can. Just listen to me. Soft, seductive and dangerously calm, the woman's voice growled at the back of her mind. *Let me guide you through it, or we can both watch them turn each other into chopped liver. It's your choice, darling.*

Pain ripped through his body, forcing the change into being; clothing tore and shredded, until nothing remained but fur and claws. Craig. He wasn't going to get away with this. Threatening him, questioning his right to tell Simone the truth ... just who did Craig think he was?

An alpha.

One who could challenge his authority to lead the pack.

Tonight that would end, even if he had to sink his teeth into Craig's throat and tear it out. Taste the blood, the flesh of another of his kind. Almost unheard of.

Except when it came to fights over leadership and mating rights. Then the rules ceased to exist.

Two sets of fur-covered bodies hit in midair. Teeth snapped at his form, new pain lancing outward from the bite. It should have knocked him on his ass, but he didn't care. It was time to show the bastard just what he was stepping into. Too long. He'd sat back and taken Craig's remarks for far too long now.

His paws landed hard against Craig's chest, growls filling the air.

The table jolted, spilling the vase, knocking it to the floor along with the still-colorful flowers, glass cracking, shattering on the kitchen tiles.

A door. Someone opened a door.

Claws raked his sides. His teeth closed on Craig's neck. A tumble -- water. Water coated the tiles, sending them both flying. Shit. He had to get the upper hand here, or claw. It didn't matter, just as long as it kept Craig away from Simone.

His mate, not Craig's.

His choice in female, not this upstart's. Not the bastard that pushed at the edges every chance he got. Foolish. He should have dealt with Craig years ago.

Focus, you fool. Don't let your anger rule you. Not in this shape. You know the price if you lose control.

Didn't they all?

An eternity trapped in the form of a wolf, never again able to walk as a man. Those days of the full moon turned into something else. A beast, the cross between man and wolf that had spawned the legends of the vicious unthinking, rabid creature that humanity thought his kind to be.

So don't let it happen. Keep your focus. You have to keep that from happening. Imagine what she would think of you, this new female, this mate you wish to claim, if you lost control. You'd be no better than a cub.

That he could never permit.

Pain lanced through his side, claws biting into his flanks.

He turned, almost in midair, snapping at the throat of the one who sought to challenge his right to rule the pack. Wood scraped along the floor, the table jarred from the impact with a lupine body.

One small part of his mind questioned the sanity of fighting inside the house when the door had been opened and wondered about the mess that would be left behind, the repairs he would be forced to do.

The rest cared for nothing but bringing Craig down. Pinning him to the floor and teaching him a much-needed lesson.

Chapter Twenty-Three

Listen to me, not them, not the fight. Listen to me if you want to make this work. I've been doing this for a long time, since before you were even a mote in your mother's eye, so focus on my words. I can help you through this.

She nodded, trying to shut out the noise. Though why she was listening to a voice in the back of her mind ... no, it made sense, in an odd sort of way. Had that been the source of the buzzing earlier? Did he have a voice, an advisor?

Where had she got that idea from?

Pack memories. Yes, you all have one. Now focus. Every part of you is alive. You can feel it, sense it, the pulse of life through your veins, power that you never knew existed until now. Every sensation threatens to explode, to take control of your body, but you can ride it out, be the one in charge. You will rule it; it will not rule you. You have the strength to see this through to the bitter end.

Her hands clenched, nails digging into her palms, pain so mild yet cleansing. Strange. Pain had never been cleansing before.

That's it. You get the idea. Now your body. Let the change wash through you; accept the gift of the earth. Claws, tail, fur ... such soft, warm fur. Stretch out, feel the wood of the deck beneath your paws. Arch, howl your pain, your delight to the sky. The moon is out. Let it welcome you as you now greet it.

It hurt. Hell, it hurt. A living fire danced from limb to limb, arcing through her muscles, tearing into her body, forcing her to assume a shape alien to her yet so very seductive. She wanted this, needed it, in a way she had never thought existed. With a low moan, she reached for it, embracing the fire in her body.

Clothing tore under her own nails, her body shuddering as she dropped to her hands and knees, feet still bare. No, not hands and knees, paws. She had paws, a tail, and a wonderful lupine form.

Scars

A cry, a howl of delight and agony both escaped, greeting the moon as it hung large, whole and pale in the dark country sky.

She was a wolf.

"Go!" Steve's voice broke through the last lingering remains of her pain. He reeked of need, lust, and a hunger she now understood. "Move away from the house and call to them. They'll listen. Dammit, you've almost got me wanting to shift now."

She didn't wait to be told a second time, but turned and bounded down the steps to the pasture, calling out to the two males as they scuffled in the kitchen. They hesitated but a moment. Then they stopped fighting, turned, and followed her out of the house, answering her summons. He'd been right. They couldn't ignore her.

Of course they can't. They're male and you're a female in heat. Did you seriously have any doubts?

Doubts, all her life she'd been plagued by them.

Things had changed. She'd changed. Men listened to her now. They wanted her, both in this form and her real one.

Are you sure that your human form is your true one?

No, she didn't have an answer to that.

Two sets of growls, challenges. Her would-be mates fighting again. The dirt tore up beneath their paws.

You want to stop them, to step in between them, yet you don't. The thought of them fighting over you is exciting.

Of course it was.

You're taking a risk, a big one. It could backfire on you, big time. You need to focus. The fight has to be stopped.

Why? Wasn't this the way of things? The males would fight, and then she would choose the one she wanted to be with.

Ah, yes you've been listening to him, haven't you? That nonsense of one mate for the female, yet the males can have fun with as many females as they desire.

She frowned. What did the voice mean?

You're werewolves, not true wolves. The whole one-male-per-

female is nonsense. One they've been quietly encouraging for generations, but think about this. If they can have extra females on the side, and everyone's okay with that, why can't you have extra males?

The fight almost faded as the words formed at the back of her mind. Good point. Why couldn't she have more than one? Though what she would do with multiple men in her life, she had no idea. One was more than enough, too much at some points in her life. Especially if they were like Kyle.

These are not men like Kyle. Get that through your head right now. These are chosen, blessed beings who can match you, be with you, and you like them both. Don't you?

Did she?

Craig, responsible for the marks on her face, yet so full of life. Could she ever look at him without recalling the pain of that night?

Victor, who set her body and heart aflame with a drive she had tried to hide for too many years.

One she was meant to be with, yet she wanted both.

What sort of a woman had she become that she wanted two men?

An alpha of the pack, a woman, a wolf, neither yet both. You can have anything you want. Just as long as you don't let them dictate your path to you. Be the strong woman you know you are, that you were always meant to be.

The fight. How could she sort out anything between them if the fight continued?

A sound. A car, a new one? Who would be coming in at this time of the night? More of the pack? How had they known?

The same way Craig had.

She danced back out of the snapping teeth of one of the males. Uncertain for now as to which one was Craig and which was Victor. She should have been able to tell the difference between them.

Scars

You can, by their smell. Just use your common sense. Well, wolf sense.

Scent, of course.

The car stopped, bodies piling out. A woman, one man, metal glinting in his hands, eyes harder than flint, a too perfect face. Kyle.

How?

What in hell's name was he doing here?

Later. She'd find that out later. Metal, a gun, shotgun maybe, no time to take the chance. With a low howl she turned, sprinting toward the treeline. They had to follow her. She'd have the chance to explain things to them later.

Steve, Paul, she could hear their voices; they'd deal with Kyle for a bit, long enough that she could get the two other wolves away from the danger of the gun.

Why weren't they following her?

She turned, arching her neck, lifting her head toward the night, howling from the depths of her being. Come. Come now!

Still snarling, snapping at each other, they broke away from the pasture, sprinting into the treeline with her. Good, at last. Men. So easy for them to become wrapped up in their own little disputes.

Could a female wolf hit two males over the back of the head with a two-by-four?

Only when you're in human form, and I recommend the double-handed grip approach.

Chapter Twenty-Four

A noise, a car, scents of people as they arrived. One he knew; the other had a faint air of familiarity to it. It all merged into one for a moment. Craig snapped at his flank as he tried to find a way to sink teeth into Victor's body. Victor growled, turning on his hind legs, dodging back out of the way.

Damn him.

Craig still wouldn't back down.

He snarled and darted forward even as Simone intervened. He wanted to ignore it, but her howl, the power of her voice in lupine form, was a cry he couldn't ignore and neither could Craig. Without a word, they separated out.

Where in hell's name was she going?

He frowned, focusing on her retreating form.

Move, now. She's got the right idea. The man has a gun; he'll see you and shoot. Go.

A gun. The stranger had a gun. How dare this man enter his home, his place of safety, without permission. Coward. Armed and threatening those under his care. His pack.

Okay, you're angry. Deal with it later. We have to get clear of here. Now. Go. You've got to follow Simone.

With a low snarl, he turned and ran toward the edge of the trees, barely aware of the other wolf at his side. She called. His mate wanted him, wanted him by her side. The stranger with his weapon might seek to hurt them all, to kill the pack.

Not something he could permit to happen.

Moonlight filtered through the trees, soft patches of pale illumination leaving a silvery caress across the forest floor. Low sounds, human voices. Steve and Paul were doing their best to keep the stranger from following them into the treeline.

Why had he come?

Why the weapon?

Scars

Questions to be answered another day.

His gaze fixed on the she-wolf. Simone. She was beautiful, strong, and graceful as she stood there in a clearing, waiting for them, with her full, thick fur, long tail, and glowing eyes. No wolf could ever want for more in a mate. He'd take on the world if it meant being at her side.

A ripple and reality split, fur stripped itself from her body as she shed the seductive lupine form and rose to her feet. Naked, standing in a patch of soft moonlight, Simone cast a calm and collected gaze over the two wolves.

"Well, are you going to stay like that, or shift so I can actually talk with you?"

Odd, she should have felt cold or ill at ease as she stood there before the two wolves. She didn't even have a stitch of clothing to cover her body, just the moonlight and her hair. All those years of hiding her face, her body, faded away as she watched the two shed their beast forms and return to being men.

Two very handsome and completely naked men.

She'd seen Victor like this before but that didn't stop her from enjoying the view. Taut lines, curves, the faint traces of old scars across his stomach and chest. She smiled, letting her gaze linger on the outline of his cock, a smile that grew as his flesh hardened, rippling into life.

Swallowing hard she forced her gaze away.

Craig, just as naked, stood in front of her. Tanned, thicker about the neck and arms, a series of long, claw-like scars marked him from left shoulder to right. She tried not to follow the path of the marks, but couldn't help it. The temptation was too great. Like Victor, he'd reacted, his erection stiffening into life.

Did werewolves have the option of taking two mates?

According to the voice she had suddenly acquired, that was an option. One the two men in front of her wouldn't want her to think about.

You'd enjoy it. I know you would. They are rather delicious-looking, now that I come to think about it. All you have to do is persuade them that it's for the best.

Right, they'd sit down, have a few cups of coffee, and start sorting out living arrangements. What in god's name was she thinking? Craig had marked her, and now would see her separated from Victor, given half the chance. The two men would struggle to work side by side; the idea of mating them both was out of the question.

Why? You just have to beat them over the head a few times. Actually you do have an ace to play. They won't remain faithful to you; why should you be bound by rules that neither of them would be willing to stick to?

Good point.

Her thighs pressed tight together, heat rising between them, her sex rippling, clenching on air. A dozen images of being trapped between the two men flashed through her mind, one mouth on her neck, the other nibbling down her back, two sets of hands moving over her body. Kissing, stroking, parting her until she felt them both thrust into her body.

"I think she's got other things on her mind than conversation." Craig smirked, leaning against a nearby tree.

"It takes a while to get used to the primordial drive the shift brings." Victor glanced at him, then back at Simone. "Though I wish we had something to throw over you, love. I'm having a hard time controlling myself here."

"This isn't the time or place for that." She tried to sound forceful, but failed. His hands, her body, the soft earth beneath them. No, focus on something else.

"Oh, I don't know. Sex in the moonlight?" Craig brushed one long finger over his chin. "Not saying I would be able to restrain myself from joining in, would be a tempting sight, but wolves don't share mates. We don't mind using the other unmated females in the pack, but mates -- that's a whole different ballgame. Pity that."

More than a pity.

"Ah, I see. So you two are fine sharing in some ways, but if I wanted to have you both, then it would be out of the question? Not exactly fair, is it?"

"Nope, but that's the way it is." Craig shrugged.

"Why?"

"Well, it's the way it's always been, that's all." Even in the shadows under the trees, she could see the slight frown that creased a path across Craig's brow.

"Just because something has always been that way doesn't mean it has to stay that way."

"What is it you needed to talk to us about?" Victor settled down on a stump, his gaze never leaving her form. "You did want us to change for something other than a little chat about you bedding two men, I take it?"

"The man that arrived. I know him." Better than she knew many others, even Victor. She knew every dark facet of his being, the anger and the cruelties he was capable of. "It's Kyle."

"Who?" Craig frowned.

"The man she left." Victor's shoulders stiffened.

"The man that beat and raped me until I learned how to pull away." Simone felt her hands tighten into fists at her sides. "For too long I let the marks you gave me force me into some stupid mistakes. You gave me the marks, but I made the choices. I don't like what I did, but I can't blame you for it. Not fully. Not even to a small degree." She'd made the choices, then been too afraid to step away when the small signs of a man quick to strike out had changed into a full blown violent temper.

"I'm -- I'm sorry." Craig's face drained of color. "I never thought. It's just that I wanted you back then and thought ... Shit. I never meant for it to turn out that bad." He slid down the side of the tree, settling his back against it. "I really never meant for this to happen to you."

He just saw his mate-to-be and tried to do what a lot of youngsters do -- push before it's time.

Men. It didn't matter if they were normal humans or shifters, they were prone to making the same mistakes. Being fair, the same could've been said about women as well.

His mate-to-be?

So there was a chance that she could persuade them that two mates for one woman might work out. If she wanted an ongoing headache.

Now I thought that was an excuse you used to avoid getting laid.

"It's over, in the past, or it will be as long as Kyle stays out of the way." Kyle. He'd had no real reason to follow her. Unless she counted the fact that he didn't like it when a woman laid down the law. She'd broken away from him, left without his permission. Dammit, how had he found her?

Simple enough, she still had a few letters forwarded to her from home. All it would have taken is one letter left behind, or an old envelope.

"Why would he be here? I can understand him following you out to your cabin, but here?"

"Ann, the woman with him was Ann. I'd know her scent anywhere." Craig glanced up.

"You've fucked her often enough." Victor took a step toward him.

"Hey, I'm entitled to let off a little steam now and then, and it's not like she wasn't willing."

"And that makes it okay?" Victor pushed to his feet. Craig followed suit.

"Cut it out, both of you. We don't have time for this." A piece of wood, a decent-size branch, and she'd be able to smack them both over the back of the head. "You two can do the alpha male standoff thing later. Right now I'm more concerned about why they're here."

Scars

How Kyle had found his way here had to be Ann. And the why? Because the bitch had led him here to find her. Revenge.

Good, you're catching on.

"Well, if he wants you, he's going to have to go through me." Victor turned his gaze back toward Simone.

"And me. Sorry, but if he's going after our alpha, then you're not standing alone." Craig smirked.

"And you're both going to stand up to him buck-naked?" One delicate eyebrow rose, a smile twitching the corners of her lips. "That will be an interesting sight to see. Hate to break it to you, but he's not into men. He likes women, vulnerable women."

She could see him -- closed fists, eyes blazing, spitting obscenities in her face. Everything had been her fault. She'd lacked the skills required, the type of beauty needed to keep him faithful, unmoving in bed. All those lies he'd used to try and turn her into the compliant, submissive creature he enjoyed. Simone shuddered, wrapping her arms tight about her stomach. The bitter taste of bile was at the back of her throat as she fought to keep from throwing up.

"The type of woman you used to be." Victor strode toward her, cupping Simone's cheek in one hand. "A woman you no longer are, Simone. You're stronger now. Strong enough to face anything he tries to throw at you."

"I know."

"So what do we do now?" Craig glanced between them, his voice still quieter than it had been in some time.

"We face them. We walk out of here, and we face them down. Ann and Kyle. Find out what they want, what's brought them here, and we don't take any shit from them." She smiled, rolling back her shoulders, her gaze moving from one man to the other. "They're on our ground, and we handle them. Any way we have to."

"This is nuts. He's armed." Victor's jaw set, his lips pressed into a tight thin line..

"And we can watch for that. Hopefully he won't even hear us walking up until it's too late. Not as if we'll be alone, either. Paul and Steve are both up there, having it out with him, from the sound of it." The raised voices carried easily through the cool night air, arguments dying, only to burst back into life. "He wants to see me; she wants to see Victor. Let's give them exactly what they think they want."

"You're mating this one?" Craig nodded toward Simone.

"Yes." Victor smiled.

"Then we're both crazier than I thought."

"It's beginning to look that way, isn't it?" Victor smiled. "And don't try telling me you wouldn't swap places in a heartbeat if you thought you had a chance."

"Heh, true enough. Given even a small opening, I'll steal her from you. Okay, so are we doing this?"

Males. Doesn't matter what species, they're all the same when it comes to an outsider stepping in on their turf.

Victor nodded toward her. "It's up to the boss here."

"Let's do it." Damn, it would have been easier if she'd had clothes on though.

Chapter Twenty-Five

"Well, well, now. This is an interesting sight." Kyle turned, taking in the odd scene, his grip on the shotgun easing as his gaze moved over the three of them and then lingered on Simone. "Not one I had expected to witness, but I'm not going to deny that now you've made me very curious."

"What in fuck's name is going on?" Ann's voice rose an octave or two, panic touching her eyes. "You're naked; you're all naked. Why haven't you got any clothes on?"

"You noticed. And if you're not aware of the fact, this is my home and my land. If I want to run around buck-naked, I can. So can those I invite onto my property." Victor smiled, sitting back on the edge of her car. "I thought you'd been waiting a long time to see me naked. You've been trying to get into my pants for how long now? Four, five years. No, let's be brutally honest, since you turned old enough to notice men. So get a good long look; it's the only chance you're going to get."

Ann's face darkened as she turned and looked back at Simone. "You've all been fucking around out there, haven't you? You've been out playing around in the trees with that damn slut."

"Are you sure you want to call me that, Ann? How many men have you been with? I'd say at least two today. Craig and now Kyle." Simone spoke softly, shaking her hair over her naked breasts. "You don't have to lie around us. You love sex. Nothing wrong in that, just as long as you hold everyone else to the same standard. If I'm a slut, what makes you think you're any better than me?"

Victor didn't try and hide the smile, or his pride as Simone spoke. She'd nailed it, the scent of sex mingled with Kyle's scent was obvious, at least to his kind. The smug smile from Kyle only confirmed it. Damn the woman. Did she have to spread her legs for every man that walked in?

Only if they have something to offer her, money, power, a way to push you and Simone apart. Craig was the same, a way of getting to you.

"How dare you." Ann paled.

"I'll dare a lot more if you don't get your skinny ass back in your car and get out of my sight." Simone's voice never rose above a calm, steady tone. "You're really not wanted here. Not right now, at least. Oh, and something to think about. I've spent most of my life being called one name or another, so if you think throwing words like slut or bitch at me is going hurt me, then you've really no idea the true cruelty of the man you brought out here. For that you should count yourself fortunate."

"I was never cruel to you, lying little shit. I treated you the way you deserved. If you'd been a real woman, one who knew her place, then everything would have been fine between us." Kyle smiled as he spoke, yet no light touched his eyes. A dangerous man, one that might snap if they pushed him too far.

You won't lower your guard around him, neither will Craig or Simone.

No, out of all of them, Simone was the least likely to stumble where Kyle was concerned. She knew just what he was capable of.

"Craig, you can't just sit back and let her treat me like this, after all we've been through together." Ann half reached out for him. "I thought we had something special between us."

"Don't look at me for support. I happen to agree with her." Craig shrugged, folding his arms across his chest. "Sure, you're a decent turn in the sack, but it doesn't make her a liar."

"Bastard, you total bastard." Ann blanched. "How can you do this to me? After all the times we've shared. Those days you came to me looking for a little company. I never turned you away, never. Now you turn on me. You're heartless."

"Yes, and your point is?" The words didn't even faze him.

"I don't want to see you hanging around my mate again." Simone nodded toward Victor. "He's mine. I'm his. You stay out of our lives. No more little games. No more trying to get into his bed. Is that clear?"

"Your mate?" Kyle and Ann spoke as one.

"What in god's name do you mean, he's your mate?" Ann turned on her.

"Just that. Stay away from him. And Craig as well. They're off limits to you for now. Perhaps if you behave long enough, I might let you spend a little intimate time with them just as long as you remember your place."

Hmm, she's latched on to that word pretty quickly, though I'm sure you'll explain to her soon enough that as your mate she will have to back down, from time to time, and listen to you as the lead male of the pack.

Yes, she had and the look on Craig's face spoke of issues that would have to be dealt with once Kyle was out of the way. Did she not understand that no female had the right to tell a male who they could and couldn't spend time with?

Ah, but she didn't exactly forbid you two, did she?

No, she'd issued orders to Ann. Interesting. Another problem he would have to sort out.

You need to deal with this situation, or something a little different arrangement-wise will need to be accepted by the pack. I'm not sure I like where this might lead. She's trying to push things. Changes we aren't ready for.

What changes? Victor wanted to pull her aside and find out just what was going on, but now was neither the time nor the place.

"What the hell are you talking about? You're mine. You've been mine for years, Simone. Did you think I was actually going to just let you go? I say when things are over between us, not you, never you." Kyle's gaze had fixed on Simone.

Victor's hands tightened, nails threatening to shift into claws. The urge to slash them across Kyle's face grew by the moment. No, quiet, let her handle it. She was doing fine, stronger than she had ever believed, with more at her fingertips than Kyle knew.

"It's over, Kyle. It's been over for a long time." She smiled, giving a slight shrug.

Kyle moved without warning, closing the distance between himself and Simone, one hand reaching out for her throat, tossing the shotgun to the floor.

Time moved in slow motion, Victor's hands threatening to shift into claws, teeth elongating behind his lips. He had to keep her safe, protect her from Kyle.

Too late.

Kyle's hand closed on her throat, but only for a moment.

Yet it was still a moment too long.

She growled, one hand closing on Kyle's wrist, twisting it, stepping back from the grip as she forced his hand up behind his back, one arm locking about his throat. A strength, the strength of their kind, now showed through. No matter how Kyle struggled, he couldn't break free from her grip. She just added a little more pressure to the grip on his wrist, until his back arched. Her voice now little more than a low snarl. "Don't you ever dare try and lay a finger on me again. I'm not yours. I've never been a piece of property, and I don't intend on becoming one now."

"You're hurting me." He whimpered. "Let me go. I don't like this."

"Good, now you know what it feels like." Her arm tightened about Kyle's throat, flexing. "Now get out of here, before I show you just what it's really like to be on the receiving end of the sort of crap you've dished out."

He stumbled forward, hands hitting the dirt, face pale and drawn. His eyes turned dark, lacking reason, his hand reaching out, closing on the shotgun. "You bitch!"

Hunter!

Kyle turned, lifting the gun, aiming it at Victor's mate.

"No! Simone, look out!"

Chapter Twenty-Six

Moonlight glinted off the barrel of the shotgun. There was clear, pure fury in his eyes. She'd seen that before. The danger she had experienced far too many times with him. Almost to the point where she'd expected this. Strange thing about men like him, they became predictable. At least in some ways.

"Do you really think that's going to change things?" Things had changed, at least for her. No more fear. It didn't matter that he held a gun, that he could kill her if she made the wrong move. She wasn't the same woman who had curled up in a ball, frightened, in pain, trembling as she waited for the next blow. But he was still that cowardly bully, and she was done backing down to creatures like him.

"Get down on your knees and beg." The barrel didn't move away from her. "I want to see you on your hands and knees, pleading with me for forgiveness. You know what I like, where you belong, so do it. Do it now."

"Simone." Victor, though she didn't dare take her focus away from Kyle.

"Shut up. Shut the fuck up, or I'll pull the trigger. So help me, I'll shoot if you don't shut up, pretty boy." Kyle blinked, the gun in his grasp wavering away from her for less than a moment.

Pretty boy. Now that's rich coming from him. He's proud of his looks, isn't he? I can see that, taste it on the air. Might do him good to have a few claw marks. A bite or three. Though make sure you kill him if you do that; he'd make a rotten shifter.

Tempting thought.

"I told you to get on your knees, slut."

"Why, so you can feel like a big man?" Calm, as long as she kept calm he'd be off balance. "I'm sorry you can't get off unless you've got a woman groveling for you. Is that what you made Ann do? Did you get her to pretend to be afraid of you, or didn't you care?"

Dangerous ground.

"I'll shoot."

"Go ahead. I'm not going to kneel for you." She shrugged, tracing her fingers over her body, cupping her breasts, her gaze never shifting away from him. "You miss this, don't you? You miss having me under you, sobbing, trying to shut you out as you take what you want."

His fingers tightened on the trigger, then relaxed, his breath coming in long slow gulps, sweat forming across his face. "Yes, and I told you, I didn't give you permission to leave me."

"And why would I need permission?" Could she do this? She had to.

"Because you're mine. You'll always be mine."

"Are you sure about that?" Push a little more and she'd be able to move. "Remember when you used to do this?" She pinched lightly on her nipples. "Only you used to pull them so hard I'd cry out."

"You liked it, or you wouldn't have stayed as long as you did." He smirked, licking slowly across his lips. "Gods, you squirmed so nice, hot and wet on my cock."

"And you want that power back."

"I'll get it back. You're coming with me."

"No, I don't think so."

"What? You can't say no to me; you've never been able to say no to me." Yes, there it was -- the uncertainty.

"I'm not going with you, Kyle. Not now, not ever. I don't belong to you. This is my home, with Victor, Craig, my friends, my family. Not with you." Her hands fell away from her breasts, nipples hard, tingling. "And I've said no to you before. I left you, or don't you remember that I walked away? What are you going to do with me, force me into the car with you? How long will it take for Victor to call the cops?"

"I don't ..."

Scars

"And then what? They'll come looking for us, for you. I'll stand out, a naked woman held at gunpoint in the car. Or would you try and make it across the state line? That's felony kidnapping, I believe. A long time in jail when they catch you for something like that."

The gun lowered a fraction, his grip faltering. "You don't ... I couldn't ... I won't go to jail."

"Oh, are you sure of that? Isn't that where kidnappers are sent? Jail, I mean." A dangerous game. Push him too far, and he'd pull the trigger. Maybe not on her but another. Victor, Craig, even Ann. No, she had to keep his focus on her, no one else, just her.

"Kidnapping. It wouldn't be kidnapping; you want to go with me. It's where you belong, at my side." The barrel lowered a little more. "We both know that."

"If I did, you wouldn't have to force me at gunpoint, would you?" Plant the seeds; force him to look at the situation.

Careful, use all your senses. The fear, the doubt, we can smell it on his skin, coating him. Think about it. Use the skills you now have to make sure you don't end up hurt.

Right.

She inhaled slowly. The advisor was right. Fear, doubt, uncertainty all mingled with open sexual need. Ann, she could still smell Ann on his body. Interesting.

Now, keep that in mind as you deal with him. He's short-fused. He will attack, strike out at you rather than lose you. Keep an eye on the gun in his hands.

"Stop talking; you're trying to confuse me. Just shut up." The words ran one into the other, voice shaking, his grip barely keeping the shotgun in his hands. "I can't do this. I can't let you walk away from me, but I can't -- I won't -- go to jail. You're mine. Why would I go to jail for taking something that is mine?"

"Is that what I am, a piece of furniture, or a car that you reclaim? Somehow I can't see the police believing that one."

"No, I mean ..."

"Then put the gun down, Kyle."

No one moved, or spoke. Silence wrapped around her in a heavy cloak. She didn't dare look away from him, from the gun that he still semi-held in his hand. After all those years, even now that he was armed, she wasn't afraid of him; she finally wasn't afraid of him.

"No, I'm going to have you, with me. In life or in death." His fingers tightened on the trigger; the gun raised toward her. A soft click, the trigger pulling back. Damn him, why couldn't he take the out card when he was offered one?

All she could think was, why hadn't Kyle grabbed a pump action instead of the break shotgun? At least then she'd have had a little more warning.

Chapter Twenty-Seven

Victor's muscles tightened, jaw clenched, fur, teeth, claws forced into existence. The change hit him fast, hard, and unstoppable. No one was going to harm his mate. No one. Not even if it meant exposing them all.

Simone!

Blood. He could smell her blood.

Gods, no. If Kyle had killed her, his death would be one that the pack would retell for a hundred generations.

Victor's paws struck Kyle in the chest; the gun jerked upward, a noise breaking through the air, deafening him. His ears rang from the noise, disorienting him. It didn't matter; he'd kill Kyle for this.

Meat.

Metal hit the ground, a dull sound through the endless ringing that blocked his ears. Bare throat, enticing, calling to him, pulse throbbing under skin, just a moment and it would be over. Thick, rich blood would gush over his tongue, down his throat, and the man would be gone. No more threats to his mate, no more guns waved in her direction.

Hands tangled in his fur, yanking him backwards with one arm locking about his throat. He clawed, growling, arching to twist free.

"Victor, no. She's okay. Don't give into it!" A man's voice, one he knew. Craig. Not that it mattered. He needed to be free of this. Taste it. He could almost taste it, the man's blood. The attacker's blood.

Flesh parted under his claws. A cry. The right noise. Not the right person.

More hands, tighter grips. Who?

He growled, arching, lashing backwards with his paws, a snarl as he broke free, launching himself at the prone man. Throat, so close, tempting. Time to end it.

"Victor, no!" Her voice. Alive! Gods, she was alive. How could that have been? The shotgun had gone off, and she'd been so close. Not just that but her blood still tainted the air.

He turned his focus, moving away from the shaking man, searching.

Simone. His Simone. Alive, standing up, shaking but standing up. Gravel had left scratches on her flesh. Her hands skinned ... the blood from that source? He searched her, looking for some sign of a deeper injury.

Nothing. At least not that he could see right now. Just scratches.

How?

No, that didn't matter right now.

"I'm fine, just shaken, that's all. Back away from him. Come back to me. Don't lose yourself to the beast within. Control it; don't let it control you." Her voice, so sweet, concerned. What had her so concerned about his behavior?

Dammit, can't you see how close to the edge you are?

Blood, he could smell it. Hers, Steve's, was that Craig's as well? Had he done that? Not to Simone, but the men?

His stomach rolled, knotted and rolled again.

Tempting. I can smell it as well. It would be so easy, wouldn't it? To just bite into him, tear that pretty little throat open, teach him what it's like to be the one without control. He came after her, your mate, your pack. He would deserve to die.

Simone.

Even the most reasonable of voices faltered under the pressure of instinct, the blood, the threats, and the dangerous creature that had entered their world. His world.

He needed to die, this dangerous intruder.

She'll understand. Bite into his throat, tear it out, taste him as you end his life.

No, she wouldn't. He had to change back, regain human form. So very tempting, just a small taste of him; it wouldn't take but a moment to end the man's life. Slow, sluggish, the change didn't want to come, the wolf refusing to be bottled back up, still craving the taste of Kyle's blood. He was in control, not the beast. He was.

The heady taste soaked the air, tempting him.

No. He couldn't, wouldn't give into this. He ruled the change; it did not control him. Dangerous. Seductive, the call of the beast within. It was a summons that, if obeyed, would have him throwing aside all of his remaining bonds with humanity, until he became locked within the form of the wolf for the rest of his life.

Simone. If he obeyed the summons, turned his back on being Victor, then he would lose her.

Paws became feet, his body shedding the fur, pain no longer an issue. In his rage, he'd barely felt the normal effects of the change. It had been lost in the need to destroy.

"Monsters." A soft, shaky voice. "You're a monster, a beast. You tried to kill him." Ann. Great. How were they going to handle this? And Kyle?

"I'm no more a monster than the man you brought here tonight, Ann." Craig slipped past him, picking up the shotgun and then slipping the safety back into place. "And a monster would have killed your new friend here. Nothing could have stopped someone that was really a monster. Victor stopped."

Simone's arms wrapped about his body, naked, warm, and willing. "It's all right."

"You're like him? You're all like him?" She pressed back against the car. "What are you going to do to me?"

"Nothing." He struggled to find his voice. "Nothing you don't want us to do to you."

"I don't understand."

"What are we going to do with them?" Simone murmured against his ear. "We can't just leave matters like this."

No, they couldn't. "I need to think and get out of the night air." Gravel lined his throat, scratchy, sore, reluctant to let him speak.

"Get them inside. Ann, go into the living room. Steve, get our trigger-happy friend here inside as well, but tie his arms. I'm not going to take any risks." Craig took over smoothly, flashing a smile back at Victor. "Well, we're in this together, aren't we?"

Amazing. It takes a naked woman, and a man with a shotgun, to finally get you two to work together. Why didn't I think of that sooner?

Chapter Twenty-Eight

In near-silence they walked back into the house, the only sounds coming from their steps and the occasional whimper from Kyle. Without stopping to ask questions, Paul escorted Kyle and Ann into the living room, giving Simone the chance to calm down.

Did the men share some telepathic connection?

Victor turned, a shaky smile touching his lips as he opened the door into his bedroom and started to dig out clean clothes for them both.

"Craig, here." He tossed jeans and a T-shirt at the other man. "These should fit you."

"Thanks, I'll go see what I can do about keeping Ann calm." Craig pulled the jeans on quickly. "And I don't trust Kyle."

"Understandable. Thanks." With that he was gone.

Maybe he knows you need a little extra time to calm down with Victor?

That was always a possibility.

She glanced over at Victor, her gaze lingering on his toned form.

She didn't want to leave his side, not even when they were getting dressed. Fear and concern dictated her actions in equal amounts. Those small lingering signs of madness, the beast rage that had claimed him for a short time, still showed brief glimpses in his eyes and in the way he moved. Would that happen to her at some point?

Only if you shift in anger, or extreme lust. Then you could lose yourself to the wolf. No, I don't suppose that's a very fair explanation. You don't lose yourself to the beast; you lose the ability to shift back. It all happens too fast, with no control. You brought him out this time; if you hadn't been here then he wouldn't have been brought out of it for a long time, if ever. But we were lucky, he loves you too much to walk away from you.

Strange in some ways. He denied that emotion for years yet now it saved him. Males. I'll never understand them, not as long as I live.

"We need some time together, soon." He pulled her close, murmuring into her hair, strong hands moving over her body, cupping her ass. "I need you."

"I know. I understand now, but I also have to find some time to go home. There are things I need to look into, like how Kyle found me. And there's more, the fight -- you frightened me."

"With how I changed?"

"Yes, I thought I'd lost you when you didn't answer me at first. When you tried to kill him, it was as though you weren't really there." She nestled against his chest, taking in his scent, the feel of his arms wrapped about her body. Gods, it would have been so easy to push him onto the bed, straddle him and draw his thick, hard cock into her body.

Sex and violence. There's a link between the two, you know.

Great, so every time either he or Craig got into a scrap over something and she was around to witness it she'd deal with a need to ...

Yep, don't forget it will happen when you've had a close call with a fight as well, or been in the middle of one. It's not just them.

"I wasn't." His fingers tightened on her body, painfully so, only to ease again. "I lost myself, in the change. Or came close to it."

So much to come to terms with. Would he think she was nuts if she told him about the odd voice in the back of her head?

No, he wouldn't; you all have a guide, a wolf guardian. You're coming into this late. If things had worked the way they were supposed to, you'd have been brought into the pack as a teenager, but ... your father. Well. It's not something we could risk.

Her father. Another set of questions. She couldn't hide this from him, not with how fast she had found herself pulled into this thing with two men who wouldn't have given her the time of day only a couple of years ago.

He knew and didn't want this life for you.

Scars

Knew? No. That didn't make sense. He'd have said something.

A rare few know. He did because of your mom. She carried the bloodline. You carry it. He knew the one that wanted her. It's a long story. One of love, lust, two men falling in love with the same woman. She chose your father and gave up the life she could've had with the pack. Love can be the strongest of emotions, far more so than lust, or anger; it's a driving force. One that cannot be beaten back. Love brought him back to you. Remember that.

"We can't wait much longer here, not with our guests waiting in the next room." Strong fingers combed through her hair, sorting through the tangles. "I'm not sure what we're going to do with Kyle and Ann, but we can't kill them. As much as I'd like to rip his throat out, it's not an option."

"No, it's not." She didn't want to step out of his arms, not just yet. What would happen if she did? Would he turn back into the raging beast she had seen earlier? "We'll figure something out."

"We could turn Ann."

"What?" That made her move, if only so she could look at him fully. "Are you out of your mind? Turn her? I thought you said I was the only female around that could work with the pack?"

"You're the only one who can be an alpha. She's a prime prospect for an extra female, which would relieve some of the tension in the pack."

Color drained from her face. "Oh, gods, you don't mean she'd be ..."

"If it was something she wanted and she has a taste for ... well, being friendly."

"Being a slut, you mean."

"A human term. Males need release. If a female is willing, then I wouldn't count them as being a slut. More in touch with their needs, a little like you can be with the right man."

"But you goaded her, at the party, here, other times as well. Besides, I'm nothing like Ann. I can count on one hand the number of men I've been with." Of all the things to say, to even remotely suggest that she was like Ann.

Why not? You're both female. And there's nothing wrong with enjoying the company of a male when the need hits.

"I'm still part human." He shrugged. "And there are going to be points in my life when that human side clicks in harder than other times. I shouldn't have said some of the things I have to her, but it's done now."

Ann as a member of the pack and with the ability to shift shape. Ann making love to her mate.

"I won't let her near you."

"That's not really much of an issue. We're going to finalize the mating between us. Once that is done, neither of us can be with another on a permanent basis. Wolves mate for life. What she will be is not a mate, but a pack bitch, a female willing to spend time with other males, and it might help teach her to focus. Find a better path for her life. Now, that doesn't mean I won't take a turn with her on occasion, but sexual release and mating are not the same things. Craig will enjoy having an extra female around as well." Victor tugged his shirt down, glancing toward the door. "I know, it's not the best idea, but it's one that the pack has been talking about for a long time now. We're going to need extra females. This will keep her from reporting us and will help her realize why she can't come after me."

"Now I'm confused. Sex is okay, but mating isn't." Her head hurt. This was all far more than she had been ready to deal with.

"They aren't the same thing." He smiled. "Yes, I know, human females tend to look on them being one and the same, but they aren't. Mating includes offspring, a lifelong commitment. Sex is just that. A nice time shared between those of a like mind."

Her stomach rolled. Extra females, women willing to please the pack. The thought made her ill. What other choice did they have? Ann wanted the company of men; she loved the company of men. The pack would welcome her, and Craig would as well.

It's part of life, not something to be ashamed of. And besides,

Scars

you'll get used to it once you've been a part of the pack for a month or so. Not that they'd be too happy if you sported with a beta male or pack male. They're odd like that.

Double standards. Some things never changed.

Of course, but hopefully we will be able to make them see sense. You would work well with two mates, companions, or whatever name you guys figure out for the arrangement. It will take some time to sort out, but we will sort it out.

She hoped so.

"What about Kyle?" All she wanted was a little alone time with Victor, to do whatever it was that would complete the mating between them. She shivered, her sex tightening, memories of the brief time they had spent together in the pasture replaying again through her mind.

"We'll figure out what to do with him. I'm not going to let him get away with the stunt he pulled. I don't like predators on my turf. Non-pack, ones at least."

"Is it wrong to want him dead?" The image was so tempting. It didn't take much to understand just why Victor had come close to killing the man.

"If it was I wouldn't have been able to pull out of the change. Wanting someone dead and actually seeing it through are two different things. If I'd killed him I would have become the monster, but wanting him dead ... nothing wrong with that."

He brushed his fingers over her cheek. With a shiver she leaned into his touch. Slick heat, a throbbing need rushed through her body; she could smell it -- the scent of her own desire. So could he. Craig would have done as well. So many things made sense now that she had a glimpse of the new abilities the change had brought into her life.

"I don't know what to do about him."

"Leave him to me," he smiled, slipping his arm around her waist. "We shouldn't keep them waiting any longer."

Chapter Twenty-Nine

We might have a problem with Ann. I'm not sure she's going to settle into the pack; you saw how she reacted to the idea of the other bitches.

It was part of life; she'd become used to it. They all did. Besides, she wouldn't pass up the chance of the life that was offered to her, not once it was all explained.

Or she won't adapt, and you'll have a problem on your hands.

No, she'd adapt. He had to believe that. Ann was a survivor.

Kyle. Now there was the problem. He couldn't kill him, or maim him; that would've brought too many questions their way, and turning him was out of the question.

If it weren't for the fact we need extra females, you'd be saying the same thing about Ann. Even as a beta, she'll be sniffing around you, waiting for a time when she can get rid of Simone. She wasn't raised within the pack and doesn't understand that forcing Simone out of the picture would not be possible. It would make bringing Ann into the pack a very dangerous game.

Simone was stronger now than she'd been before, and she could protect herself from a power-hungry newbie. Couldn't she? If not, he'd take care of it.

No, you won't. Females of the pack sort out their own hierarchy. If she lacks the ability to do that, then the alpha will quickly become a beta and you could find yourself in a very odd position.

She'd have the strength.

He pulled her close, nestling into her hair for a moment, inhaling deeply. Vanilla. Sex and vanilla mingled, coating her skin. It would've been so easy to just curl up with her on the bed, explore her form under his fingers, his teeth holding her throat ... No, they had work to do.

Reluctantly they headed into the living room

Scars

Ann and Kyle sat at opposite ends of the same long brown couch, neither one willing to move, or speak just yet. He didn't blame them; they'd both been shaken. A man had turned into a wolf before their eyes. Not something they could've been expecting to witness.

"Well, now, what are we going to do with you?" He settled down in the large padded chair, pulling Simone into his lap. "We can't just let you wander off on your merry way, not with what you've seen."

"Oh, gods, you're going to kill us, aren't you?" Ann whimpered, her eyes wild, tears glistening as they threatened to spill down her pale cheeks. "Please, Victor. Don't do that to me. I swear I won't tell a soul. I'll do anything you want. I just don't want to die."

Her fear was intoxicating.

Focus. Yes she's afraid, but she's not your prey.

"We're not going to kill you; we're not like that." Simone spoke before he had the chance to. "We're trying to figure out other choices we might have."

He frowned, squeezing softly on Simone's waist. He was the pack leader; it was his job to deal with this, not hers. How many years had he run the pack without her help? Now here she was trying to step into his shoes.

Hey, how often have you complained about the workload?

That was different.

Sure it is. Now bite your pride and get on with the work.

"There's one option for you, Ann. Make you one of the pack." Simone smiled.

"What?" Ann tensed, almost jumping from the couch.

"And me? What will you do with me? Will you turn me into a monster as well?" Kyle looked up, his gaze narrowing, a harsh look entering flint-like eyes. "I won't do it; I won't be one of your kind."

"We wouldn't have you in the pack." Victor met Kyle's gaze calmly. "You'd be an omega, less than that. We don't beat our females. Some are submissive within the pack, but ones like

Simone are alphas, leaders. Betas are those who are second rank in the pack and answer only to the alpha. Then there are pack females who are willing to please any male in the pack, but even they are never beaten or degraded, the way you treat women."

"Hold on. Are you saying if you turn me into a wolf, that I'd be able to ..." A light touched Ann's gaze. The fear faded quickly.

"With those that want to, yes. You'd have the right to turn them down, but I don't think that would be an issue with you, would it?"

She flushed, her thighs pressing tight, hands clenching on her lap, her gaze moving over the men in the room, though it avoided Victor. The idea appealed to her. More than that, she'd taken in Simone's warning to keep away from Victor. Good. That would make life easier in the long term.

"And I'd not have to marry ... err, mate anyone?"

"No, pack bitches don't normally take mates unless an alpha chooses them and wants cubs." He watched her closely, the focus around her eyes, hands tense then relaxing on her thighs, the soft twitch of her hips. "It's rare for an omega to move up the pack ladder, but it's happened. Normally it happens when an alpha male of the pack, one who isn't leader, wants to push out on his own and form his own pack."

With Craig that was always a possibility. Unless he still had his sights set on Simone, which was far more likely.

You two are going to have to learn to live together and more than likely share Simone. Yes, I know you don't like that idea, but once this business with Kyle is finished, you'll be able to sort that out among the three of you.

"You still haven't said what you're going to do with me." Kyle shifted on the couch. He was a mess. His shirt was torn from the scuffle, mud in his hair, nails broken, scrapes on his face. He'd heal in time, but the blow to his pride would be the telling point.

"Well now, we could turn you over to the local cops." That would have been the easy answer. "They don't take kindly to your sort."

Simone tensed in his lap, a sharp indrawn breath, her gaze seeking out his face with a silent question.

"You'd do that? But what about what I've seen." Kyle's gaze narrowed. "Isn't that taking a huge risk?"

"You forget something here -- all the other witnesses that saw you attack Simone, pull a gun on her, threaten to kidnap her, and then try to shoot her. How many here will repeat the same story whilst you try and convince the sheriff that a werewolf attacked you?" He shifted Simone on his lap, pulling her head back against his chest. "They'll tell how you beat and terrorized Simone during your relationship, and how, when she fled here, you followed her."

"They'd never believe that; there's no proof."

"Yes, there is." She spoke quietly. "I had a friend of mine take pictures with dates of the last few attacks. She's got copies herself and with a lawyer. And as I told you the day I walked out on you, there are medical records. Every punch, scratch, and cracked bone is on record."

"You conniving little bitch. You set me up. You worked it so I'd be open to this. How could you do this to me?"

"Insurance, nothing more. No one forced you to attack me. You did that all by yourself." Simone didn't move from the safety of Victor's arms, despite the harsh words that Kyle sent her way. "You caused the problem, and I just kept a record of it."

"And you're willing to run the risk of me talking about all this?" His hands tightened into fists, shoulders shaking, his jaw clenching. "You really think you're ready to take that risk."

"Why not? You know what we can become, and how many are going to believe you?" Victor smiled, running his fingers through Simone's hair. "A mad story about a pack of werewolves living out in the country? They're going to assume you're drunk, insane or you've been reading too many bad horror novels. And they're going to ask you, if the story is true, then why did that group of -- what did she call us? Monsters, that's the word -- why did a group of monsters just let you go instead of ripping you to pieces?"

Risky. If he tells the right person, one of those hunters, then we could be dealing with a major set of problems. Are you sure we can't just kill him?

Hunters. No one had seen a real hunter in over a generation. They had become nothing more than a campfire story for the younger shifters.

And most don't believe in shifters. Besides, all it takes is one.

Killing him wasn't an option.

You know that sometimes you're all too human for your own good.

Maybe he was, but he wasn't about to change. Not just to be rid of one man.

"And you'll just let me go?"

"Yes. In fact, Steve will drive you back into town. Minus the gun, of course. Then he'll see you beyond the county lines."

"I see. Then I don't think I have any other choice, do I?" Kyle's gaze shifted from one person in the room to another, then back to Victor.

"Yes, you do. You could refuse, and we could turn into the monsters that you already believe us to be and finish the job once and for all." He smiled, standing up, setting Simone down on the chair. "It wouldn't take much. A low growl, the shift into a new shape before my claws tore your neck open. We wouldn't bite you, of course. We wouldn't want you to become one of us."

Oh, I hope he says no. I really want to see the insides of his throat.

Chapter Thirty

A risk. He'd taken a huge risk in offering Kyle freedom, but what other choice did they have? Simone watched in silence as Victor handled Kyle, pride warming her body. This man, this wonderful man who wanted her at his side, had more courage than she had ever thought possible in a human being.

"Agreed." Kyle nodded. "I won't speak of this. Just don't turn me in to the cops. I couldn't face doing time."

No, someone like Kyle wouldn't last a week in prison.

"You leave, tonight. You never step foot back in this town. Is that clear?" Victor pressed the point home. "I see you, or any member of the pack sees you, and it's over. There are far more of us than you could ever guess."

How many more?

The pack is a decent size, twenty or so with more coming of age. With luck we'll find some more pack females in the coming months. You and Ann won't be enough, and with you being an alpha, well, only Victor and Craig will try anything with you.

Two men. She still wasn't so sure what to do about that.

Who said you have to rush into making a choice?

Victor, or rather he had implied as much.

Are you ready to take a mate? Victor can't answer that. Only you can, and you've been through hell of late. If you need to step back, to take a little time before you accept a mate, then tell them that. Enjoy your time. You have so much to learn about being a shifter, a werewolf, and you can't let them push you into a hurried decision.

"See him to the edge of town, Paul."

"What about me?" Ann shifted on the couch. "You really want to make me into one of you?"

"Honestly, I'm not entirely thrilled at the idea, but they have a point. You enjoy the company of men, the males of the pack need new females, and as you wouldn't be bound by the need to form a mate bond, I can see it working." Simone spoke before any one else could. "But if you cross me, I'll make you regret the day you were ever born. In the pack, I'm the alpha, not you. Is that clear?"

"Very," Ann whispered.

"Good." Simone nodded. "Then I think I've said my piece."

"Craig, take Ann home. Paul, get that piece of trash out of my sight and our territory."

Steve left with Paul to see Kyle out of town and out of the county. Craig went with Ann to begin explaining the ways of the pack to her. Only when everyone else had piled out of the living room did Simone breathe a sigh of relief. Tires crunched a slow path away from the house, the cars moving out, leaving Victor and her alone in the house.

"I wasn't sure you'd be able to pull it off." She turned, resting one hand on his shoulder as she followed him out into the kitchen. "And I had to admit sitting in your lap felt a little odd, right but odd at the same time."

"The mate of the lead male in the pack has to listen to him, stand back when pack matters are being handled. You get to sort out the problems with the females in the pack." He glanced back at her, closing the screen door. "I know you don't understand that yet, so I'm not upset with you."

"What? Isn't that a little old fashioned?" Upset with her? For not being the quiet woman letting her man deal with matters? Oh no, she wasn't about to step back and become one of those again.

"It's just the way it works. Don't worry. The only male in the pack you have to answer to is me." He pulled her into his arms, running his hands down her back, soft, light touches that left her shivering. "It's how things work. How it's always worked."

"It's wrong." She growled, nuzzling at his chest, taking in his scent. "Men aren't better suited to rule than women."

"Can you hunt? Do you know how to bind a pack together? Can you smell who would make a good beta, which male or

Scars

female has the potential to be an alpha for the pack or branch off to start their own?”

“That’s not fair. I’ve only just been changed -- how can I have such skills without the time to learn them, or learn how to use them?” She pushed back from his hold, an ember burning in her stomach, the need to strike out at him, prove she was as strong as he was. Man, woman, it didn’t matter. She could learn whatever she had to.

“It’s got nothing to do with being changed. It’s a gift few have, and only males. It’s how we’re made.” Victor sighed and walked back into the kitchen to perch on the edge of the table. “I didn’t mean it to sound harsh, but we’re creatures torn between logic, the ability of man, and the call of nature’s laws.”

Nature’s laws. Foolish.

No, not foolish, but a part of your life. Something you will come to terms with when you’re ready to. Now, though, now you must focus on learning about your potential mate. You must prepare to take your place in the pack. Even if you’re not ready to confirm the mate bond, you still have a lot to learn from him and about him.

“I’m sorry; it’s just so confusing. I know what I need to do; I can hear it, sense it. But it fights against everything I thought I knew. I get away from Kyle and his belief that I should be submissive to him, then fall for a man who says I have to listen to him and obey him in certain things.” Her stomach knotted, tearing her in two. His mate, his wife, his woman, hunting partner, mother of his children, yet her mind screamed against it. No, not against it, but rather the rules that came with the life she now wanted. “Then, there’s Craig. I don’t know what to do about him or the way I feel around him. It makes no sense. I should hate him, but a part of me wants more than just a casual friendship, or pack bond with him.”

You want him, then you must be prepared to live by the rules, the laws of the pack. It’s the price you must pay. Nothing in life comes without a price.

"I know, or I think I do. Though I don't understand why you would want to be with Craig in any form. You have the alpha wanting you, needing you. Why would you ever need another male in your life?"

"Why would you need time to sport with a few pack bitches?"

"That's different."

"No! There's no difference."

"You're female; I'm male. Of course there's a difference."

"Is that all it boils down to? The sexes?"

"Well, what else would it be? Look, I know it doesn't make sense to you, but I've lived with the laws of the pack since childhood. Most of us have. I've never had to teach someone about our ways before." His nails dug into the wooden table, brow crinkled with a deep frown. "I might make a few mistakes along the way here, but I know one thing. I want you with me, for the rest of my life. I need you. I can't imagine life without you."

She wanted to be angry at him, about the arrogance of the pack. That a man could indulge when and where he wanted, but she couldn't. Not as an alpha female.

"You don't know what you mean to me." Victor sighed. "Gods, I sound like a lovesick teenager, but that's what happens when I'm around you. Unless I'm focused on pack matters, I lose my ability to be the man I was. All I want is you, your touch, your skin against mine."

"And Craig."

"I don't want to discuss Craig right now. I want you. I came too close to spending the rest of my life without you. If Kyle had been a better shot, or moved any faster, then you'd have been taken from me. I couldn't live with that."

Life without his touch, his kisses, his scent wrapping with hers. No, the thought left her cold to the core. "Nor I."

"Then we work this out together, if you'll let me help you. Even if that means I have to accept Craig as a part of your life." Tension rippled through his body; his hands clenched at his sides for a moment. "The pack won't like it, but if that's what it takes, so be it."

Simone nodded, moving to him, wrapping her arm tightly about his waist. The shirt did little to shield the feel of his chest under her cheek. Soft, tender touches slid over her back, upward toward her neck, caressing in light circles beneath her hair as she shivered, pressing into his arms.

All thoughts of Craig vanished.

A handful of hours had passed since he'd shown her how to love, how passion could claim her body, mind and soul, and yet she craved his touch again. Cloth caught beneath her nails, his shirt. She wanted the feel of his body, not the clothing that now shielded him from her sight.

"Please." She murmured, pressing her lips to his neck. "Let me taste you."

"How?" A tremor ran through his body, breath catching in the back of his throat as her fingers moved to his pants, opening them.

"You'll see." She'd never wanted to do this for Kyle, or any other man. But for him, yes, it seemed right. She needed to know every inch of him, his taste, his scent at different moments, the strength of his body and the weakness that claimed him at that moment of release. He growled as she lowered herself between his thighs, lifting his cock from his pants, lips closing on the head of his thickening erection.

"Gods." A firm grip tangled into her hair, tight, hard for a moment, easing as her lips slid down over his flesh. "I love you, my mate, my Simone."

Her eyes closed, lips moving down over his cock, tongue wrapping about his throbbing shaft as she suckled. Trembling, she slid one hand down, circling the base of his cock, squeezing, releasing as she licked over flesh made hard by his own desire. His hips twitched, a rock that pushed him deeper into her mouth yet still held back. She could feel it, sense it, the struggle of passion she teased to life with her soft nibbles, and the tender caress of her seeking tongue. He struggled between need and the desire not to frighten her. Did he think she feared he would become the beast?

No, the danger of that had passed.

She'd set the pace this time.

He groaned, nails scraping over her neck, gripping her shirt, thighs tight on the edge of the table.

She pulled back, tracing her lips over his cock, licking the head slowly, tracing light lines over the shining purple skin, swollen with need. Her gaze was framed by thick lashes as she looked up at him, taking in the soft shiver, his lips parted, his eyes closed. A deeper moan filled the air with the soft scrape of her teeth over his cock, her tongue wrapping back about his shaft, fingers gripping, releasing, stroking as she suckled a path slowly downward.

Her cunt tightened, slick with her own desire. It wouldn't have taken a moment; she could've pulled him down onto the floor, straddled him, taken him into her body with a cry of her own delight. Soon, she'd welcome him into her core when the time was right.

Heady pre-cum coated the head of his cock, calling to her, urging her on. With a low growl she took him into her mouth fully, struggling not to choke as his cockhead touched the back of her throat. Gods, she wanted to take him deep, but she couldn't. She hadn't learned how to. For a moment she balked, torn between her need to please him and her fear.

Whimpering she pulled back, licking her way upward to his head, suckling hard on his cock. Each touch, each lick of her tongue, teased a low cry from his lips.

"Now." He growled, grasping her hair, pulling her away from his cock. Bare feet hit the floor, his pants falling to the ground as he pushed her against the table. One hand stayed tight in the soft tendrils; the other tore her pants away, kicking them across the floor with his. Her body pressed against the wooden table. "I want you now."

A moment's fear, a struggle she couldn't ignore, her hands pushing into the table as she tried to free herself from the grip that held her in place, a fear that died with his touch between her thighs and a gentle caress against her soft depths.

"You need this as much as I do. I can smell it on you, the drive, the need that binds us. Mate. Lover. Mother-to-be, when the time is right." One finger pressed between her lower lips, brushing over the tender bud of her clit. "So hot."

She burned, her thighs trembling as he parted them further. Breasts pressed tight to the table, nipples hard beneath her shirt, ass bare to his view. Soft, teasing, his fingers slid over her ass, stroking, one hand deep between her thighs, a finger easing into her sex, pressing against her core.

Tap. His finger pressed against that hidden spot.

She jerked, head raised from the table, a low gasp as shock rippled through her body.

Tap. He played quickly with the hidden source of pleasure her body kept within her core, stroking it, circling, tapping again until her body threatened to turn into liquid heat under his fingers. Her knees weak, teeth grazing her bottom lip.

"Please, love, please ... I can't wait." She'd been able to fight it back when her lips and hands had been busy on his body, but now her body ached, her sex tightened with the need to be filled by his cock.

"You can, and you will." He leaned forward, biting lightly into the back of her neck. "You'll know what it's like soon enough, to be completely mine. What it is like to run at my side through the night, greeting the moon."

Pressure built between her thighs with each light tap against her core. Her body no longer her own, tension built, her legs refusing to work as they were claimed by a deep tremble. She groaned, hips rocking back toward him, nails digging into the wood, inner thighs damp.

"We'll run together, hunt together, work as one."

She groaned, pushing toward his cock, seeking his touch.

"I can hear it, in your breath, you'd give anything to feel my cock slide into your pussy now, wouldn't you, to fill you."

"Yes." She whimpered, back wet with sweat, her hips rolling back toward him.

"Name yourself my mate. Swear to be with me until death."

She arched, trying to regain a measure of control, only to lose that last grip. Wrong. This was wrong. He was pushing things. Trying to force her to make the choice, to commit to him when she wanted time to think it through.

Of course he is. He's an alpha.

"Victor." A moan of protest in the form of a single word.

"I know you want him as well, but I can't allow it. Not as a mate. A lover, yes, not a mate. I'll grant you that."

And if she wanted more than an occasional lover?

He rocked against her, teasing.

Gods, she needed him.

And he needs you to commit.

What about Craig?

A lover, a companion, it's a start. If the pack is to change, then you have to adapt, take some small steps. And you want him.

Yes, she did.

"Yours, always yours. Until death and beyond. Your mate, yours, Victor. Yours!"

"Mine." He growled, pulling his finger from her core, his cock sliding in deep, hard, filling her. Heat mingled with pressure. Her hips slammed against the edge of the table. His fingers grasped her waist as he drove into her body. Claiming her. Taking, filling her, his cries joining with hers. Breath coming in short, harsh gasps from the both.

Blood raced through her veins. Sweat stung her eyes, blinding her. It didn't matter, just as long as she reached that moment of bliss with him.

"My mate, my bitch, my love." He growled against her back, thrusting deeper into her core. Bitch. It should have stung, but the word only pushed her further into pleasure. Wolf, female werewolf, a bitch, his.

"Yours." A scream, not a word. Her hips rocked back, hard, fast, meeting each drive into her sex. Her body craving each touch he would grant her. Slick, her muscles tightened, claimed him, holding him close, a thirst for more that only he could quench.

"Let it go." His teeth sank into her neck, biting hard and deep.

She cried out, throat raw with the animalistic noise that gained life, fueled by the fires he released to wash through her body. Muscles tightened, pressure built until she feared she would go mad, her hips rocking back, only to lock in place. Her cunt tight, slick, closing hard on his cock as she screamed only to leave her shaking, coated with sweat and need.

His growl joined with her scream, his cock pulsing against her walls, filling her twice over until he dropped down against her back, unable to keep upright any longer.

"Mine."

"Yours." Light danced before her eyes, spots that blocked her vision. Her legs were no longer willing to answer her commands.

Peace. She'd heard the word, knew it could exist as a feeling, even glimpsed it from time to time. But now she understood it. He'd brought her peace.

Epilogue

Leaves crunched under her paws, moonlight summoning her through the trees, leading a silvery path into the darkness of the treeline. The wind that tugged at her fur was soft, cool, and welcoming. Trees, damp grass, rotting leaves mixed with the dry ones, all beckoning her further into the night.

How many years had she feared the darkness that lay beyond the windows, or shuddered, hiding deep under the covers if she heard a dog or wolf outside, and been left wondering if they were going to come in through the window again?

Nights wasted in terror, fingers clutched at the blankets, even when she'd been living in the city with Kyle.

Never again.

No more fear.

She had nothing left to fear.

Could she forgive Craig? A part of her already had.

Attraction. She felt more than that toward Craig, but she'd made her choice, accepted a mate.

Ann. A problem of a different calling. They'd go head to head, the same way she knew Craig and Victor would in the months to come. Still, she was the alpha, not Ann, never Ann. Just as long as she remembered that, Ann would be kept in her pack-assigned place.

A noise, soft, a warning of a paw on the forest floor, his scent carried on the same breeze. Mated, hunting together, time where she could run with him, enjoy the freedom of her new form.

She was stronger now, perhaps with new life already growing inside her womb. His children. They'd be born human -- he'd explained that much to her -- but they'd know what it meant to be raised as a part of the pack. A family, an odd, twisted family, but one that would never let her children face the hatred she'd known, or fall prey to the type of man she'd wasted too many years with.

Scars

Packs looked after their own.

No more thoughts of the past were needed. Mistakes. Everyone made them. Human, shifter, it didn't matter; being a werewolf or whatever other strange creature existed here gave no protection from walking into bad relationships unless you had someone else to turn to for advice.

Now she had that.

Long and low, his howl broke through the night air, calling to her, summoning her to his side. A howl that was joined by a dozen others. Dark forms slipping through the retreating night to meet with their leader, to greet their new alpha female ...

Terri Pray

Terri Pray is a stay at home wife and mother currently living in Iowa with her second husband. She was born in England, only moving to the States in 1999. They have two children together and share a love of writing and role-playing that brought them together via the Internet. Together they not only run a chat site, Dark Fantasy Chat, but also work in the RPG industry and Terri can often be seen at such conventions as ValleyCon, Gen Con and Origins at the Final Sword Production booth.

Visit Terri on the Web at www.terripray.com.

Scars

www.ingramcontent.com/pod-product-compliance
Lightning Source LLC
Chambersburg PA
CBHW050538190726
48284CB00003B/1122